Winter Dance Party

Advance Praise

"*Winter Dance Party* is a wild and wise collection of fever dreams set in an ailing Iowa. Brett Biebel's down-and-out denizens are compelling kooks you can't help but love. These are short stories bursting with big lives."
—Ryan Ridge, author of *New Bad News*

"Brett Biebel's debut collection, *48 Blitz*, called to my Nebraska heart, and I've followed him ever since. He's upped the ante with his latest collection, *Winter Dance Party*, where he deftly answers two fundamental questions: Why do we cling to history, and is progress always a good thing? Always present in these 59 stories are the ghosts from that night in 1959, when the music died in Clear Lake, Iowa. The characters we come to know in *Winter Dance Party* feel the spectral pull of the past in their bones, as they love and fight, give the middle finger to big business and big developers, and often struggle simply to find something or someone to hold on to. Biebel masterfully weaves parentheticals throughout many of these stories, paying homage to how many middle-America oral storytellers constantly interject seemingly insignificant bits of exposition in their tales. But they're not insignificant. We meander, we divagate. But pay attention, because we're connecting the dots of our intersecting lives, culminating in the human collective. East and West Coasters think there's something different, something a little off, about those of us in Flyover Country. Biebel is here to tell you we're not so different. In fact, we're just as aimless and disconnected, yet always grasping for more, as the rest of you."
—L Mari Harris, editor of *Trampset*

"Brett Biebel's *Winter Dance Party* is an incredible glossola-
lia of haunted voices. His characters speak in tongues and
dance in the flames of a still-burning plane crash—each of
them febrile, sweating, panting—and his prose is as psychi-
cally infectious as rock & roll. This is the Midwest as you've
never seen it, and Biebel's sophomore collection is better
than you can possibly imagine."
—Barrett Bowlin, author of *Ghosts Caught on Film*

"*Winter Dance Party* encompasses the Buddy Holly plane
crash, the roadside attraction, how it affected people in the
surrounding area, and how it continues to do so. The characters are your neighbors, the people you see around town,
learn about through gossip, or encounter one strange night
in a bowling alley or empty field. You get to know them
throughout the loose ties of the stories, weaving your way
through the cornfield and the parentheticals inside of parentheticals that read like whispers in your ears. In this
book, Biebel's deft writing captures the obsession and mys-
tery surrounding pop culture history."
—Allison Renner, author of *Won't Be By Your Side*

"In *Winter Dance Party*, Brett Biebel takes us on a nostalgic
1950s musical journey through the Midwest in prose that
sparkles with the melody of sunsets over cornfields. These
flash fictions take us back to an era of optimism cloaked in
ash and chemicals. Biebel writes with urgency and pathos,
putting us in the boots and tuxedos, the aprons and hair-
nets of these humble characters, risking it all for another
kiss, inhale, drink, or soft touch between hours of manual
labor and the desperate yearning to live well or die trying.
Biebel moves from satire to realism, to the wacky and un-
containable, with stories pulsing with life and verve! I
know these people, and still I read to find out their secrets.
Biebel in language and craft doesn't disappoint!"
—Tommy Dean, author of *Hollows*

Winter Dance Party

Buddy Holly's Crash Site in Flash

Brett Biebel

Alternating Current Press
Boulder, Colorado

Published by Alternating Current Press
Boulder, Colorado 80302
altcurrentpress.com
All rights reserved

Library of Congress Control Number: 2023942316
ISBN-13 (paperback): 978-1-946580-34-4
ISBN-10 (paperback): 1-946580-34-1
ISBN-13 (hardcover): 978-1-946580-35-1
ISBN-13 (ebook): 978-1-946580-36-8

Interior and cover design: Leah Angstman
Author photo: Meg Kunde © 2023

The following is a work of fiction created by the author. All names, individuals, places, items, brands, events, characters, &c., are the product of the author's imagination, are used fictitiously, or are entirely coincidental.

Printed in the United States of America

10 9 8 7 6 5 4 3 2 1

Table of Contents

Buddy Holly

Ritchie Valens

The Big Bopper

For my whole family . . .

"And no one knows we're anywhere we're not supposed to be, so stay awhile and watch the wind throw patterns on a field."

—John K. Samson, "Winter Wheat"

Buddy Holly

Field of Dreams

When Royal Treatment Properties bought up the Buddy Holly crash site, they said nothing. Refused to send out a press release. They left untouched the big novelty glasses out on Gull Avenue and paid an old farmer more money than he'd ever seen to pull weeds near the makeshift memorial, to make pleasant conversation with tourists and locals and whoever else happened to come on past, and the whole idea was to keep things quiet. "Keep it normal, keep it quaint," they said (in intraoffice emails and after-hours conversation at HQ in Minneapolis), though that didn't stop a few Cerro Gordo County busybodies from catching wind of the whole thing, and you know how Iowans are. The old ones, especially. Soaked in nostalgia and ready to resent any kind of change (particularly one involving deeply rooted local traditions), and it wasn't long before people started asking questions.

Mostly, they wanted to know what use a development firm (with resorts all over the Great Lakes) could possibly have for an empty field miles from anywhere, and they figured it had to be something awful (a suspicion that only got heightened when some disgruntled ex-RTP employee leaked a memo talking up "the next Midwest vacation destination" (or, as some in the C-suite referred to it, "The Dells in the Dirt," or, in one case, "Disneyland for Death Nuts")), a nightmare high-rise or swimming pool complex or waterpark, and one of those "concerned citizens" groups (which always include the nosy neighbors and small-time thinkers and crazies out to lunch (as well as some (presumably) decent people)) passed around fliers that claimed RTP wanted to build a sprawling and "basically sacrilegious" tourist trap on the very site of the plane crash, complete with chalk outlines in the lobby (for Buddy Holly himself), at the bottom of a proposed waterslide (Valens), and in the middle of the ground-floor Honeymoon Suite (with the Big Bopper's feet sticking out from under the bed). Only part of that was true, of course, but that didn't prevent the formation of a groundswell of concern, enough that some 400 people showed up to a meeting of the county zoning board, and the courthouse was so packed that they (meaning the entire board) had to reschedule, to move the whole thing to the Surf Ballroom itself, and they (meaning the entire board) promised to let every interested party speak before reaching any decision, which meant the whole thing lasted nearly nine hours. They had to take breaks. Dispatch volunteers for cookies and lemonade. Every so often, they'd fire up low-key (50s era) background music, and people would discuss commercialization and economic development and pieces of history. Someone (who smelled like vodka and wet dogs) said he'd never seen any of these people at other meetings, and maybe they were all from Des Moines or St. Paul and only bused in to make the whole thing look controversial, and then someone accused him of being the out-of-towner, of being on RTP's massive payroll, and this was the moment of highest tension, the moment of physical confrontation, when two strung-out guys (neither of whom was part of the initial dispute) in a booth sponsored by the Clear Lake Super 8 swung wildly and then wrestled around on the floor. A girl (who couldn't have been older than 20) asked about a rare species of cricket and the importance of environmental protection. RTP chose a woman to close the meeting on their behalf, and she wore leggings and reading glasses and said nothing could be more in line with the spirit of Iowa than this very project. She locked eyes with each board member in turn. Gestured (on the advice of a well-known consultant) all around the room. She looked like a young Susan Sarandon, and she said people would be desperate. That they'd make pilgrimages. Play license-plate bingo and count cows and horses and graveyards, and, when they arrived, they'd hand over the money without a first thought, let alone a second, and you folks are already on the map, but this is going to make you a destination, and all we have to do is build it, and people will come. People will come, Ray (and here she made sure to stare at the ceiling and look open and steady and glazed). People will most definitely come.

Lighthouse Inn #6

Days I spent at the Surf Ballroom, waiting around for girls. Sometimes I read books about war or football or how to succeed in business, and sometimes I just sat. I'd find some booth in the corner or off to the side, and the booth was always sponsored by Community Bank, or maybe the Clear Lake Super 8, and the only time it ever worked was Lydia. Or Lauren. I can't remember. She must have been 37, at least, and dancing to Tommy James and the Shondells, and when we got back to the motel, she made me wear these Buddy Holly glasses and said I should call her Peggy Sue while we rolled around on the floor and found each other's tongues. Hers tasted like coffee grounds spiked with casino liquor, and when the clothes came off and it still wouldn't work, we ordered pizza from this place called Uncle Angelo's or Cousin Billy's and sat there using the carpet as an ashtray and talking about car wrecks and ice cream and whether we had any kind of a future.

"Maybe," I said. "Probably. As long as you don't leave right this second, and let's just go ahead and see what comes."

"What's so great about a future, anyway?" she said, and so I told her, I said, I don't know, but I was always gonna end up all full and floppy beside some nowhere interstate, and maybe that wasn't so bad, and what did she think? Maybe this one could be just good enough.

Races Run

Uncle Bernie had this cat named Bronco, and he used to let it ride around in the cab of his pickup, and sometimes I'd be back there, and every time he hit a pothole, the cat would jump and hiss and sound like this woman who lived above us back when we were at the apartment, this 40-something Missus April, who drank cases of Mello Yello and smoked while sitting cross-legged on the balcony, and it was like Uncle Bernie was happy, like it was the ride of his life, and this one day, had to be around Thanksgiving, it was 15 degrees, and we pull up to that OTB used to be out past the mall, just off 35, and we leave old Bronco behind because Uncle Bernie says he's got a little birthday present for me, and I can either take it now or let it ride, and of course I want to let it ride, and so we go in and bet 50 on Rows Hoed to win in the sixth at Hialeah because this is back before it closed, and the whole place smells like tobacco and getting older, and when the sonofabitch finishes second, we scrounge together a dollar or maybe 89 cents in pocket change and get one of those fried fish sandwiches, and Uncle Bernie rips up the ticket and puts all them little scraps under the bun and then throws it in the back there with Bronco, so we can watch him go at it like he's a street cat, like he's about to face the firing squad, and my uncle says, "Fucking animals," and punches me in the shoulder, then gets this look that's real serious, serious like a heart attack, and he goes, "Kid, let this be a lesson," and, "Everything you touch is gonna turn to shit, anyway."

Dead Letters

In the obituary (which didn't even make the *New York Times*), one literary critic noted that Daniella Flores-Whitaker was "almost criminally underrated and dangerously insightful" and that her work (in particular, a 600-page novel (though some argued it was really a "collage novel" (and others said it "contained no semblance of narrative at all")) called *Title IX* (which used pieces of federal code and the text of (what Flores-Whitaker claimed were) actual sexual-assault claims filed at a small Catholic college somewhere in Iowa to paint a sprawling portrait of institutional corruption and misogyny (what Flores-Whitaker called "the fundamental and original form of American rot"))) "speaks to a level of bureaucracy and alienation seen only in Kafka and certain Departments of Motor Vehicles located in the lowest circle of hell." So, it was "no wonder," said the critic, that Flores-Whitaker died in obscurity. After all, she was depressing. She eschewed the *New Yorker*/Iowa Writers' Workshop model of narrative, of realistic literary fiction. More than that, she attacked the university (and (in what was "perhaps her most unforgivable sin") did so by villainizing faculty members even more than administrators) and therefore condemned herself to a posthumous career of nearly nothing. The obituary ended by predicting that someday, "70 years hence," all of Flores-Whitaker's work would lose its copyright to the public domain, and still no one would copy or print (let alone buy) it, and this was the ultimate tragedy, the perfect microcosm of the pervasive problems of the modern literary establishment.

Fortunately (maybe?) for both the writer of the obituary and Flores-Whitaker herself, however, this prediction turned out to be wildly incorrect. A decade after the obit came out, a group of feminist scholars on the campus of Michigan State University organized what they called the "10-Year Reckoning" (because "anniversary" sounded too laudatory, too tame for what they were "commemorating" (which involved pretty much exactly what you might think)) and included *Title IX* (the "novel") as part of a year-long reading and discussion group, and the book took off (for some reason no one could quite figure, though later critics proposed that it had something to do with its ability to work not just as a prolonged, immersive reading experience, but also in smaller chunks, in anecdotes and hashtagable moments) to the point that it became the university's "common book" (the book all incoming, first-year students read) for the next two years and then a key part of a class in postmodern literature (taught every other semester (during which time the (so-called) novel also generated followings across academia, and Flores-Whitaker studies became a respected academic discipline) by a professor whose full name was I. L. Reed) until at least the 2040s, at which point technological and geopolitical changes accelerated to the point that the book itself required entirely too much context to be useful for incoming students (most of whom were 18 and 19 years old), and it again fell out of favor, though (as if by magic) bits of Flores-Whitaker's other work came floating up out of the aether to take its place.

Primarily, focus shifted to a series of (what were originally) blogposts that Flores-Whitaker had written sometime in the 2010s that (according to her official biographer) she'd planned to turn into a book. They dealt with her experiences as a lifelong Green Bay Packers fan and tried to reconcile (week-by-week and during one glorious Super

Bowl-winning season) the tensions between her philosophical and ethical convictions and "the sheer, adrenal joy" of watching grown men smash into each other at full speed. For nearly half a year, these posts were publicly available on the web, and then they abruptly disappeared. The theory is that Flores-Whitaker didn't want them out in the open while trying to sell the manuscript, but no one can be totally sure what happened. Mostly, critics just count themselves lucky to have found the essays at all (given that the essays' existence had to be inferred by a scholarly examination of archived email and then only confirmed after a series of formal requests to (and confrontational phone calls with) the Archives & Data Storage Division at a major Silicon Valley firm (and one of the involved scholars called it "a fucking miracle (not to mention an unconscionably shortsighted moment of economic idiocy, or else a blatant attempt at academic PR)" that the drafts were made public at all)), and for a while, these essays managed to speak to mid-21st-century college students in a way that bureaucracy never could because football is king. Football is life. Football is America, or at least it was, until suddenly (maybe another decade later) it wasn't, and nearly everyone who'd played the game at a high level over the past 50 years started to look like Muhammad Ali trying to light the Olympic torch, and anything containing the barest praise of such a barbarous activity became taboo and practically blacklisted (at least within the confines of the academy).

At this point, there were those scholars who, like the author of Flores-Whitaker's original obituary, mourned (for a second time) the loss of such a linguistic force, and for a moment they tried to revive interest in her career by digging up a few pieces (many of which utilized institutional narrators (and one of these narrators was even identifiable as a private health-insurance provider with a massive market share, and there was talk of free speech and libel and transformative use and threats of both litigation and counter-litigation that never ended up going anywhere)) of very short fiction (flash fiction, microfiction, nanofiction, etc.) she'd published online and in various (and obscure) print outlets, but, even though everyone assumed they'd be perfect for a generation whose collective attention span seemed to be the size of a water molecule, the pieces never earned many plaudits (or even the barest level of engagement), and so, now, today, whenever someone hears the name Daniella Flores-Whitaker, what he probably thinks of is an audio recording. It's from a phone call she made in 2017. The tape was acquired by one of the scholars listed as essential in securing the football essays, and his idea was as follows: Companies record everything. Everyone has to call companies. That means that, somewhere, you can hear David Foster Wallace trying to order some product he saw on TV at 2 a.m., or Thomas Pynchon dialing 1-900 (just for fun, probably, for shits and all kinds of toothy giggles), or, yes, Daniella Flores-Whitaker telling a woman from Comcast to "go fuck your eyelids with a fork" over a disputed late charge, and this is precisely what the tape contains. They play it in college classrooms, and the students sit rapt. They roll their eyes. They laugh. They hear the author's voice flushed and pissed and all-fire fucking helpless (while she tries to argue about the arbitrary nature of language and time and the impossibility of ever entering into a fair contract with any entity who (by rights) can change said contract whenever "the bloody fuck" it wants and on any kind of "flimsy whim") and touch their hands to their temples, so they can do what Sue from Comcast does. Because they want Flores-Whitaker to stop talking. They want to hang up on her, too.

Now Everybody—

A man is waiting for Thomas Pynchon to die because he wants public mourning. He wants national obituaries (and for the body to lie in state). What he wants (at least) is a more recent photograph, or maybe a posthumous American Nobel, but he never stops to think that Pynchon might be gone already, not until one night around 3 a.m. (when he's dead asleep and rock hard and dreaming of something mechanical and unrelated), and once the idea arrives, it establishes permanent residency. It starts paying rent. It drives him to sell his house and load up his car and crisscross the country. New York first, then southern California, and he hits up literary (and national) landmarks all along the way (Springfield, Massachusetts, and the Delaware Wedge and the New York City sewers). At the Four Corners, he meets a woman who says she heard Pynchon was back in Mexico, which causes the two of them to drive straight to Tijuana, where they drink tequila and talk about parabolas and preterition and hole up in a motel next to an *alberga* for two weeks. Some nights they try (and are usually able) to find psilocybin. Some nights they screw and sweat and read aloud from the juvenilia because they know everything else by heart. She likes the intro to *Slow Learner*. He thinks it's just another Pynchon joke. They fight about it for a while, and then the neighbors join in. They shout for an hour. Yell out equations having to do with echoes and sound waves and the speed of voices traveling through various kinds of walls, and, at a certain point, he can't stand it anymore and leaves her frightened and screaming at his back. At his ghost, which maybe hovers there (for a few hours, anyway) while he goes wandering about the city. While he sneaks back across the border and into the waiting arms of a Captain America who shoves him into an ICE van, and together they drive for what feels like hours, and, when he gets out, he's smack dab in the middle of some kind of holding facility, surrounded by Guatemalans. Salvadorians. Hondurans with neck tattoos. He's reciting the story of Byron the Bulb when the lone Mexican says to shut the fuck up. The Mexican says Pynchon doesn't exist. He's invented. A character out of a Bolaño novel, and just as the two are about to come to blows, the agents arrive and tell our man his whole ID situation has been resolved, and he's now free to go. They give him back his clothes. Claim he never had a phone. They buy him a bus ticket to Santa Fe and tell him to go hang out with the other weirdos and hippies, and always remember he's lucky to be alive, and he does go to Santa Fe, except he doesn't stay long. He's more at home in Roswell, where he spends 40 days walking around downwind of the old Trinity Test Site and collecting isotopes in his pockets, knowing someday they'll work their way into his hips and then probably explode. On day 41, he leaves. Heads to Iowa and joins a Trappist monastery. Mostly, this is because he's out of money. He's an oblate for a year. Maybe two. Then, he swears the usual vows and drinks wine and tries to get high off incense. He meditates. Builds caskets. Goes weeks without eating and copies *Against the Day* out longhand (in calligraphy (and he thinks maybe some fellow acolyte will hear about his work on some message board and then start his own pilgrimage, and maybe there should be code words, little Kilroys hidden in the margins)) like they used to. Like they should. He holds the hands of dying monks (brothers with cirrhosis and lung cancer and heart trouble, priests who stare at crucifixes hung on bare walls and mumble about the resurrection of the body and the holy, catholic, and apostolic church). Hears confessions from pedophiles and pornoaddicts and tells the latter they didn't do anything wrong. They smile. They pray. At night, it gets quiet, and there are more stars than he can count, and the bells ring for compline, and he gets lost in the chants. The words. He thinks of Saint Anthony of the Desert and tries to get all mystic. To contact Pynchon in his dreams. It's been maybe a decade at this point, and he figures his hero (his savior, even) probably is dead by now and most likely buried in an unmarked grave somewhere along Vineland (or else near an abandoned postal route, some empty parking lot on CA-49), and Pynchon's death must've managed to escape everyone's notice, and isn't that just perfect? Isn't it exactly right? He decides it is and then all at once feels like Charles Mason going on without his Dixon, and when death finally comes for our man (while he's sleeping off (what felt like) a hangover), a massive load of dimethyltryptamine makes him think he's on some 18th-century galley (that feels oddly German (or else maybe like a rocket, a water-bound missile)), and Pynchon looks 25 in his navy uniform, and they sit there in the middle of the ocean. The ship is massive. It creaks like an old floor. Salt hits them in the face, and they are looking at meteorites and about to cross the equator.

"There are rituals," says Pynchon.

"I know," says our man, but he can't make eye contact. Can't stop thinking about his companion's teeth.

Pynchon checks his watch. They figure it's a long way to Norfolk, and maybe there are some girls below deck, and our man decides it wouldn't be a bad way to go out, and, even if there aren't any, maybe there's time enough to understand. He needs to ask if any of it means something. If this is everything. If it really will be eternity, and please, God, let this all last long enough for me to somehow figure it out.

Heavy Water
Brewing Company

At Heavy Water Brewing Company, Gripp said the future was going to taste like plutonium, and I wanted to know what he meant. This was on the patio. Outside downtown Seattle. I was drinking a Dirty Bomb while he shielded his eyes from the sun.

He said back in Idaho, back when we still had a paper, that the editor sent him out to Hanford to write about the most toxic place in America. The story was supposed to be about the Trinity Test Site. About manufacturing the raw material. It was supposed to be about the cost of nuclear superiority, or maybe the lessons of history, but all Gripp wanted to do was drink a glass of radioactive water from the Columbia River. He imagined it would taste like ash, or Tang maybe, like rocket fuel or this moonshine they used to make at La Bamba, which I think must be closed now, too. I told him, I said, seems like you never managed to do it, or else you wouldn't be here now, would you, and he laughed until he coughed. He called me a fucking idiot. He said the drinking was way less dangerous than the sneaking away, and by the time he got down to the river and back to the tour group, they'd practically called the FBI. The other reporters were whispering, and the lady in charge, she did head counts every 10 minutes for the next hour, and this old man who said his name was George kept looking at Gripp like, hey, son, did you manage to bring any back for me? Finally, Gripp just had to admit what he did and tell him no, no, he didn't bring any water back, and George begged to know what it tasted like. Gripp stalled, mostly on account of having no idea what to tell George until they got up to the old Hanford High, which is filthy and black and generally about as bombed-out as any place you've ever seen, and finally Gripp said, the thing is is it tastes sort of normal. A little like fish shit and algae, maybe, but otherwise no different than what you might get at a hotel two states over, or it could be my palette just ain't sharp enough, and George laughed at that. George said, what did you think, you was gonna grow wings? Because they say there's some guy out there who actually did, who thinks you can turn yourself or your grandson or your great-great-grand-somebody into some kind of, like, actual bird or Godzilla, maybe, and then start, like, a whole new race of human. Just keep on drinking until you become a mutant or X-Man or what have you, and I heard this guy set up camp somewhere near the B-reactor, and I have to confess, the whole reason I'm here is just so maybe I can catch a look. Gripp nodded, he said. And then spent the rest of the tour staying the hell away from George.

What do you mean, I said, and it sounds like that was the real story, right there, and why didn't you write about that? About urban legends and little atomic cults right here in Washington state?

He took a deep breath. His eyes called me an asshole. He said, you sound like my goddamn editor, and he told me I missed the lede, and this was the problem with young reporters is that our whole generation is shaping up to be a shitbath fucking waste. My goddamn editor said what they've been telling me for years, and I know you heard it, and this time it came out like, kid, you'll never amount to nothing. There's no motivation, and your whole problem is you ain't never had the guts to just put your head down and then follow your ass right on through.

The General Lee

Someone parked an old Dodge in front of the house and then left it there for weeks, and Lynette and I watched from the window while the authorities put an orange tag on the hood. "Vehicle has been illegally abandoned," it said, but the tow company must've been overloaded, or maybe the city was broke, so no one came to get it. It just sat there. Waiting to be snowed in. The windshield iced over, and we pretended it was ours and joked about painting a Confederate flag on the roof. One night, Lynette grabbed a coat hanger. I put on rubber gloves. The Dodge smelled like vinegar and Winston Reds, and I found four ounces of weed in the console, but then when we tried to smoke it, it turned out to be dragon-bud tea. So, we boiled a bunch of water. We drank the whole bag all at once, and, after a while, it felt like we were flying to Japan. Like we had on makeup and silk robes, and I asked Lynette to dress like Daisy Duke. She gave me Buddy Holly glasses. We found our way into the back seat and fogged up the windows, added a few cigarette burns to the upholstery. We drank a bottle of Karkov. Rolled down the windows and talked all night, shivering, and I could've swore we were headed for frostbite, but body heat and warm breath and liquor make up for a lot, and she told me she'd never been scared to die, and I said me neither, though it wasn't because I was raised Catholic, and we were glad we didn't have kids. It'd be just one more thing to wreck.

I think we slept out there. Or maybe we came in at

dawn. Then it was two days later, and some guy was fixing a tow line. He had on a Bears hat, and we watched him take the car away and then mourned it for months. Years. We mourned it like it was a dead relative or a dead celebrity, like it was Tom Petty or Marlon Brando or that guy who sang "Come On, Eileen."

Midnight Shift

Old boyfriend used to work the overnight at Hy-Vee, and I'd meet him in the parking lot around dawn. Sometimes I'd bring an Egg McMuffin and coffee, and sometimes it would just be chewing tobacco and Kit Kat bars, and then we'd drive on up to the place Buddy Holly died and talk about insects. We'd talk about moths. He would tell jokes about purgatory and our pal Buddy having to listen to the crickets for eternity, and then we'd grab fistfuls of dirt and lob them at each other real soft. We'd stick them in our pockets. Let them gum up the washer in some laundromat down by the cemetery, and this one time, we took a couple of pills he said he stole from a priest and just laid there. Closed our eyes. Old boyfriend said his grandad always told him he didn't have no ambition, but the truth was he had all kind of plans, and one of them was to fill these old mason jars with bed bugs and then drive on up to Minneapolis. He had a map of downtown, the suburbs, all the Fortune 500s. Figured he could get into some law firm or investment group at the IDS, maybe ride the elevator in Accenture Tower. He could find the Target building or Best Buy or even one of them upscale housing complexes overlooks the ballpark and just open them jars in the lobby. Just let the freaks run free. He figured he needed maybe five, six jars to make it worthwhile, and he'd already started a collection. Made friends with an exterminator. I must have been high because I told him I wanted in, and we could be like Robin Hood or Bonnie and Clyde, and he scoffed. Kicked dirt at my face. He said I could talk tough, but this was real shit, and some folks would even call it terrorism, and I said, yeah. Maybe. Probably. But then I found his hand, and our fingers interlocked, and I told him I meant it, that, if they call it terrorism, it's only because the assholes got the means to complain.

Hang 'Em in the Sky

Two men robbed a bank and then holed up at a bed-and-breakfast in nowhere Iowa. The place was called the Andromeda Inn, and the owner didn't believe in electric lights. He wore a mustache and said the lights polluted the air. They caused cancer. They made cars swerve through guardrails and drove whole herds of cattle insane. The rooms were stocked with candles, but at night, the two men would blow them out, then close the curtains and play Marco Polo in whispers and sighs. When they found each other, they'd grab for anything they could. Ears. Hands. Asses. Whatever there was. Whatever was there. Then they would grapple and twist and tumble into the darkness, hoping like hell they'd hit linen, that they'd land dead smack in the middle of the bed. Somehow, they always did, and once there, they'd talk about tallow and spermaceti and Cetus outside the window there and also how many candles was old Moby Dick. One of them might say something like, "It won't be long before some asshole turns us in, and maybe we should get moving," and the other would reply, "Or maybe things will be better in jail" because they would not rat. They'd end up in the same cell block, maybe even the very same cell. Guys would come in and ask for favors, and nobody would fuck with them, and they'd be kings of the joint, wild-eyed and legendary and uncivilized. Then, they'd fall asleep. Galaxies swirled overhead. They'd dream about waves on rocks and a naked woman screaming, then they'd wake up, wet and cold, sometimes holding hands.

It took maybe a fortnight for it to happen like they said. The owner, or it might have been some tenant, some sleepless drifter, some straitlaced cowboy, finally cracked. The cops pulled in around 2 a.m., and you could see the blues and reds for miles, and to this day there's folks out in Whittemore, they swear it looked exactly like the northern lights.

The men went quietly. They were loaded into separate cars. Except some rookie parked them side-by-side, and it looked like the two men were sending signals with their eyebrows, so the lieutenant stepped in and pulled one of the cars around to the back. The building faced farmland. Soybeans. The B&B owner took out the trash, and he nodded at the lieutenant. He shielded his eyes. He thought, maybe the cops'll execute them. Maybe they'll use the chair. And then stories will spread, and people get curious, and all that voltage? Maybe it ends up good for business, after all.

Eppley Airfield Honeymoon

Me and Lena get laid off on a Tuesday, and we use the severance to buy a few dozen piranhas, then set them loose up by the airport, and there's enough money left over to grab some real nice steaks and a couple cases of Coors. We bring a portable grill. We sit by the water, drinking. She throws in a few rocks, and I tell her that in 10 years we'll be seeing beavers all up and down the shore. Muskrats and rabbits and maybe dogs, even, and every last one of them will be stripped right down to the bone. Could be there won't be very much left. It's warm and after midnight, and her eyes look real good in the dark, and she's got these ripped jeans tugged down past her hips, and she must catch me staring because she says I shouldn't get too excited. What she says is them fish'll be belly-up by winter, and this all ends just exactly like everything else.

Not Fade Away

On prom night, my date picked me up in his father's Cutlass and drove us 90 miles down the interstate. I didn't care. I didn't really know him all that well. His name was Donald, but everyone called him Richie, and the whole car smelled like hamburgers and latex, and we ended up at the Buddy Holly crash site. He parked on a dirt road. There was fucking corn everywhere. We left the thing running because we figured we could at least dance a little. It was an oldies station, and I didn't know any of the words.

"Listen," he said. "They're playing our song."

"What's that?" I said.

"Whatever you want, baby."

"Okay."

We danced, and there was nobody around. He said he had some vodka in the trunk. I'd heard it rolling around back there and thought it was a bowling ball. Or an old can of gasoline.

"Someday, they're gonna build a hotel out here," he said. "Just you watch."

"So?"

"You wanna see the spot where he landed? They say they only found pieces. Glasses all broke to shit."

"I saw a dead body once. In the morgue. At Mayo. They keep them in these freezer drawers, and they all look blue, blue, blue."

"I was there, sunshine, remember? You held my hand and said, 'This is the worst kind of field trip.'"

"That doesn't sound like something I would say."

"Of course it was you," he said. "It was always you," and I thought about how men get off on feeling like they're in the movies. They all think they're just exactly like James Dean.

He asked me if I wanted to make out under the giant pair of horn-rimmed glasses, and I said I'd rather roll around in whatever place they found the Big Bopper, but he didn't happen to know where that was.

"There's this motel down in Clear Lake, though," he said, "and all I told your pops was, 'Sir, I'll have her back by dawn.'"

I looked at him like he was an insect. Or a scorpion. I heard crickets, and it sounded like they were doing it, and I pictured them eating one another afterward, but then I thought maybe that was spiders. Or crabs. Or else just kind of something else.

"Take me home now," I said.

And he did. I don't know why, but he listened, and the drive back was silent, but not angry silent. More like sexy silent. I kept staring at him, and he'd look back at me, and we'd drum our fingers and smile, and all I wanted was to turn west at Albert Lea and just take the interstate to Wyoming. To Montana. To Big Country and Big Sky and just mute and eye-fucking and flying straight off the edge of the map.

The House
on Highway 18,
Probably October 1999

When I was 12, my dad spent a week camped out in the backyard. My brother and I would bring him Hamburger Helper and these little packets of ketchup we stole from the McDonald's down the street. We'd talk about spaceships. Constellations. The night Ritchie Valens fell from the sky, and Dad said someday he'd show us where it happened, and we could leave flowers, and he'd never done it, but the drive really wasn't all that far.

Except, that fourth night, we didn't bring him anything. Could only see his shadow hunched over inside of the tent. My brother had found a dirty magazine in the dumpster behind the gas station, and we sat on his bed looking at it. Some of the pages were torn out, some hanging half off. One of them had an ad for Campari. The women looked like they were from California or Florida or someplace with lots of fruit and no snow, and my brother said someday his wife was going to look like that, and maybe mine would, too. Only uglier. With fewer teeth. Definitely smaller tits. Then he said who was he kidding, and I wasn't ever getting married, and his pal Lamar told him I was probably gay. I said I wasn't. He rolled his eyes. I watched his eyeballs moving around inside his head and realized he looked nothing like Dad, that it was only their laughs that sounded the same.

The Nightlife, Baby

I never did make it to college, but I went with guys who did, and one of them, his name was Erik spelled with a k, I think, or I guess it could have been a c-h. Tall guy. Looked kind of like a tennis player. I remember he was in this class on public health or sociology or something, and the professor gave them this assignment where they all had to sleep outside for a night, and, Erik being Erik, he decided to go for two. Asked me if I would come with. Well, yeah, sure, fine, I said, and let's make it a slumber party, and so I brought Cherry Coke and popcorn, and Erik got the condoms, and we ate and drank and fooled around under this old railroad bridge over by the creek. When it got dark, you could hear an owl. Homeless men would come by with carts. Every rattle would echo, and we weren't much inclined to sleep, but we couldn't have done it even if we tried.

On the second night, we met these two high school kids, and they asked Erik if he was holding, and he said, hell yes, and pulled out a .38. They took off like rabbits. They shouted the whole goddamn way. I watched his hands shake, and I wrapped one of them around my waist, and I said, "Do you want to move in together, baby?" and he said, "Baby, what do you think this is?"

We laughed at that for an hour, it felt like. Heard the wind kick up. Leaves and dust kept smacking our faces while we dozed against the cement. When the sun rose, the retirees came by on bicycles, and by 10 a.m., the whole place smelled like dog food, and it still does, this town. You can't escape it, and sometimes I have half a mind to try for a job at that plant out there, on account of at least that way you could get used to it. At least you could manage to forget.

I think Erik graduated. Probably got a master's. Maybe he's in Florida now, and what I do is just loiter inside the Fareway. I linger in the pet aisle. I stare at them economy bags of Purina and Iams and breathe real deep, and when I start to feel horny and lonely, I'll think, maybe it's time I should get a dog, but then I know it won't help because I'll resent him after a while. I'll spend all that money, and the poor mutt will just sit there whimpering, and an arrangement like that can only turn out for the worse.

Buddy Holly
Body Double

They say her name is Lydia or Lorraine or some such, and she likes to drive on out to the crash site in the middle of the night and find the place Buddy Holly landed, and I mean the exact geographical spot. She's got reams of old photos. A BA in physics from Wartburg (or sometimes Coe (and somebody once told me it was actually Grinnell, but his word ain't mean nothing since about 1978)), and she runs computer simulations to reconstruct the scene and the wind and the flight path, and sometimes she dresses like he did that night (only without the glasses (or maybe she's got pairs and pairs and pairs, and she just tosses each one out the window on her way over there and lets them shatter on the pavement)) and just lies there face down or face up or maybe on her side and with her fingers curled in the dirt. No one can say why she does it (hell, nobody even knows who she is, exactly), but it's got to be something to do with ghosts. With nostalgia. With Don McLean and some kind of dead America, and she figures if anyone's going to show her what it all means, it's him. It's Buddy Holly. And the whole thing makes you wonder if his DNA is still out there in that field, and maybe she's out there sifting. Panning for gold. Maybe she's got some crazy ideas about reincarnation, or maybe it's oxy or that methamphetamine or what have you, and it's got her senses all heightened because they say she doesn't do much of anything while she's there. Just listens to crickets in the summer. Crows in the winter. She closes her eyes and sleeps right where they found him for hours, through dreams about poodle skirts and sock hops and simpler times (or maybe about wreckage and fuselages and smoke), and there's a rumor going around the high school lately that says she brings men out there. Boys sometimes. Teenagers. Somebody heard them theater kids talking (and vaping, they said) near the lake the other day, and they seem to think she picks the nerdy ones. The geeks. She makes them wear Buddy Holly glasses and drags them out to the spot and then has her way with them right there, or else she makes them strip naked and sing "Maybe Baby," and then she just takes off and leaves them standing (maybe still singing) alone, excited and shaking, and it's got to the point now there's gangs of boys (and one or two girls, even (the kind with hair that's pink (or mint green) and tattoos and who're always talking about politics)), and they drive on out to the spot late at night. They lie in one of them fields across from the memorial. It's soy out there this year, and it don't provide much cover, but they probably paint their faces. Toss hay on each other. They point their phones at wilted flowers (or that wiry little guitar), and they drink (or get high) and pray like only kids can. They pray they'll catch her. Maybe that she'll choose one of them. They get all hyped up about the internet and what you call viral sensations, and there's a few probably think it'll be their ticket out of here if they can figure out the right thing to do with her once they get her on film, and some of the teachers is real worried it'll be the kind of awful that makes the national news, and one of them (probably from the English department) even went to the county (I heard the sheriff himself) herself, and they put out a statement just the other day that said they were thinking about extra patrols. They said that maybe they ought to assign an officer to Buddy Holly duty all night for a week, just in case and just to see what comes, but then the town held a meeting, and we shut that down right quick because the reality is there ain't a whole lot of political will. See, we figure there's better uses for taxpayer dollars. We figure this Lydia or whatever you call her is some kind of nut. A grown woman with a death fetish. We figure whatever she's doing out there is her business, and personal freedom's a damn fine value, but hitting up famous farmland in the dead of night never has been the world's safest bet, and if them boys ever find her, well, they probably get a good story. They get a cheap thrill. Hell, they probably get spooked and run away, and whatever happens, I guess we figure that this Lola or whoever she is knows what she's been up to. She probably deserves whatever she gets.

Land of the Blind

When he was five, I took Kenny to the dentist. The place was way out past the highway. In the middle of hayseed nowhere. We sat in the waiting room looking at cornstalks, and the man across from us was wearing an eye patch. Kenny kept gawking. I think he probably pointed, or else let out this wheezy, child-sized gasp. "Mom," Kenny said, and I mouthed, "I'm sorry," and the man half-grunted, or maybe he just kind of flicked his wrist. Kenny kept right on staring, staring like he was comatose. Out the window the corn was neck high. It must have been August. The stalks were swaying back and forth, and it looked like fingers or clotheslines, and I swear you could hear the rustling through all them panes of glass. Maybe someone was reading a magazine. I guess I suppose it could have been that.

When they called us back, the guy with the eye patch grabbed my arm. Kenny jumped half a mile. The guy said, "You tell him, lady. Tell him I got this the last time I was here, and, kid, sometimes dentists make mistakes. They drink too much whiskey. Their hands get sweaty. They're off thinking of paydays and bikinis, and they forget how to hold the goddamn electric drill." His other eye started twitching, and his grip got tighter, and it took this death stare from the hygienist to get him to let go.

Kenny started wailing. Wailed through the appointment. Wailed the whole way home. We couldn't get him calmed down until lunch the next day, and Jerry and I were bleary and half-dead, and we hated that guy more than anyone I ever met, but now it's 20 years later, and we still talk about him. We thank the good Lord. We say, where would our Kenny be without him, and most days it's like he was the best teacher the poor kid ever got to have.

Good Wood

Our neighbors got foreclosed, and the bank never came by, and so we watched the house falling down. Weeds growing up. It looked like one of them barns out in the country where it's all still standing but only just, and you can imagine bats and raccoons and whatever, and I asked Will if he wanted to go over there and mow on account of the aesthetics and all, but there wasn't nothing in it. No compensation. Property values were good and tanked, and to tell you the truth, I agreed with him, and one night we broke in there. It smelled like dog food. No different than outside, I guess, when the wind is right and the Purina plant's firing, and we got a blanket and a battery-powered radio and listened to the Cincinnati Reds, and that Great American Ballpark was full of fucking echoes, man. It sounded like our beer cans. At night. Rolling across some bullshit laminate floor.

The Silent Killer

Fillmore said he had a cousin who used to live out by the Purina plant in Davenport, and once, twice a winter this cousin'd be out shoveling snow and come up with dead squirrels. A rabbit, on occasion. Maybe a mouse. He said this cousin figured it was the rock salt or Roundup or maybe radon at worst, but he didn't think too much of it. Told the realtor when they sold the house, of course, on account of he's what you call a good citizen, but she guessed it was probably that they got stuck under the AC unit and froze or maybe some neighbor kids pulling a prank, and, either way, it wasn't worth disclosing, and then Fillmore's cousin moved, and two, three years later, the cousin's waking up with sweat all over the sheets. It's soaking through the mattress pad. He's dropping weight. His wife is begging him to go to the doctor, but he keeps saying it's nothing and then driving past the old place on his lunch break. Doesn't know what he's looking for. Maybe it's one of them radon remediation units, or maybe it's medical equipment, little glimpses of folks all bald and skinny through the windows, and all he knows is what he doesn't want to see, and it happens it's a tricycle. A swing set. Them little toy trucks make realistic sounds and run on batteries, and this cousin can live with the nightmares. That subconscious swirl he gets clear and regular, and it's worse in the winter, and what he sees is roadkill. Sulfur clouds. Methane in his nostrils, and the only thing he can't abide is kids. Is slow doom. Is 50 years of a ticking clock and the way life turns into nothing but panic, the way toys in the backyard can feel like tiny, endless kicks to the teeth.

American
Gothic Revival

I think it was June. The 22nd, maybe, and the first tourist to show up at the old Buddy Holly crash site saw three dead animals. One was a raccoon. The other was a deer. He was pretty sure the last one was an armadillo, but it took him a minute, on account of it not being native and all (though, later, after all them people showed up, one said he'd seen armadillos on the side of old Highway 6 back from when he was a kid in Nebraska, and people called him a liar, and maybe he was, but the point is it's plausible, is the son of a bitch could have been right), and the tourist didn't know this, but the animals were laying right where they found the bodies of the musicians. The raccoon for Buddy Holly (on account of the marks around the eyes, they figured), the armadillo for Valens (which a few of the college kids (on break and with nothing better to do) said was racist (and, on second thought, maybe there's something to that on account of Holly's the one from Texas)), and the deer for the Big Bopper, seeing as it was a buck. An eight-pointer. With a head would have looked nice in any cabin or supper club, and this tourist started snapping photos, but he didn't think much of it until this old farmer came running and sweating and asked him what the hell happened and did he see anyone? So, no, said the tourist, and the farmer hurried off and started making panicked phone calls and closing down the path with duct tape out near them novelty glasses on Gull Avenue, except a few locals came by (and there's people say the locals just happened to be passing through and other folks think it was organized (like, as in, they must have got bused in), and some just believe people are always going out to the site in the morning to drink or get high or screw all in public and next to death like that (on account of they say it's quite the thrill)), and they knew the significance of what they were seeing and made some phone calls of their own, and the next thing you know, half of Clear Lake and a quarter of Mason City is out there. The cops are asking the tourist questions. Poor Elaine's running the deli out at the Hy-Vee all by herself because everyone else called in sick (or maybe it ain't poor Elaine at all since I hear the store was practically deserted), and people keep whispering about what it is they're (most of them) looking at. Somebody says it's the work of that Lola again, and damn if she didn't get tired of just laying in Holly's spot all by herself, and now she's got to go and defile it with roadkill, and that story gains traction for a minute, and the police make plans to ensure Lola's safety, but then the farmer comes back, and his voice is real stoic again, and most of them folks know him, see, they respect him, and so they're apt to listen, and he says the whole thing's probably just some accident. Some kind of random occurrence. He says, hell, one of his boys hit a raccoon with an ATV just yesterday, and he didn't think nothing of it, but can't be no broader significance. No kind of divine message or nothing, and maybe we should all just take a breath. Now, these people respect him, of course (like I said), but we got lots of folks around here afflicted with that modern skepticism, and so the disgruntled ones, now they turn on the farmer instead. They ask him how he explains the armadillo then, huh? And ain't no track marks they can see, no blood neither, come to think of it, and just what are the odds these dead carcasses end up in those exact spots, and pretty much everyone admits it's pretty unlikely (and most seem to take it (meaning the exact geographic locations) for having some kind of spiritual significance), and the farmer tries to protest, but some teenager (one of them theatrical kids, I think) starts in on how he heard some famous graffiti artist (with a name I can't recall) was down in Des Moines this week, and this must be his latest project (seeing as it's the kind of thing he's known for), and then the teenager starts snapping his own pictures and making sure to fit himself in the frame. He lays down next to the deer. Someone tries to lift the armadillo, and this theatrical kid tells the guy to fuck off (and how this is art and all that (which means you ain't supposed to touch)), and the next thing you know, the cops are breaking up a fight (which they had to do at least two more times before they got animal control out there and all them corpses hauled away). Now, I ain't seen all of this personally, but I got it from folks I trust, and, later, they come to me and ask where I'm at with it, and what do I think, and should we demand they ditch that new hotel out there and all that, and I don't know what to tell 'em. Never been much for grand meanings. You do what you do and then you do it again and then you try not to die (although you know you're going to, anyway), but I'm talkative on account of the weather's nice. Sun's going down. I got a drink and a lady lives up in Manly, and so I answer. I tell 'em. I say, sure seems like some asshole's crazy. Like he don't like what's in the air out here, and he's got something to say, and the whole thing's a hell of a visual grievance, but, to me, it says just the one thing. Which is we're doing something right. And we oughta keep doing it. Whatever it is that we do.

Three Frog Night

Two weeks after Mom left, my brother and I caught three frogs out near the lake. We named them Buddy Hoppy, Ribbit Valens, and the Big Hopper, and my brother taped them to this model airplane he'd got for Christmas, like, three years before, a P-40 Warhawk. He still had some of the glue. We climbed out the bathroom window and onto the roof sometime after Dad fell asleep, or maybe he was just laying on the floor watching TV, I don't know.

"Say a prayer, asshole," said my brother, but I couldn't think of any just then, so I said the names of stars, only I didn't know many of those, either.

"Betelgeuse," I think I said. "Alpha Centauri," and then the plane was in the air. It didn't exactly fly. More like it spun and flipped like a football and rammed into this big tree we had to cut down a couple years later, and then we climbed back in through the window and ran downstairs to scope the wreckage. My brother had a lighter. He said we were gonna make a pile out of the rubble and then add newspapers and gasoline until the blaze got good and popping, and then we'd cook the frogs on it. We were going to camp out. We were going to eat frog legs, but then we got there, and we could only find two bodies. They were pretty smashed up. We looked for Buddy Hoppy for an hour, or maybe it was Ribbit Valens, but we never found him, and, in the end, we buried the other two under the tree. My brother made me dig the hole. I had blisters for a week. And the whole time I was digging, he just sat there, opening and closing the lighter and talking like a math teacher. Like a cop. He kept telling me, over and over, how there wasn't no way the other one was alive, and listen, he said, a crash like that leaves no man behind.

Pilgrimage

They say the crickets out at the Buddy Holly crash site are magic (or maybe just lucky), and people drive from Des Moines and St. Paul and Omaha (and sometimes as far as Denver or Lubbock or Reno) with their trunks (or the cabs of their pickups) stuffed full of mason jars. There are holes cut in the tops. They save their grass clippings (sometimes from watered, deep-green lawns, and sometimes from those patches of dirt and weeds that like to hang around near trailers) to spread along the bottom, and some even have these big, fancy terrariums that (in addition to probably costing a fortune) look like dioramas of the pioneer Midwest, complete with little sod houses and cornstalks and (in at least one case) actual fragments of cow shit, and when they all arrive in midsummer on coordinated "picking days," they compare notes and talk about textiles and techniques for prolonging insect lifespans. There is an artist from Chicago who's out there for days at a time, and she's got this wall of crickets set up inside a tent on Michigan Avenue, and they say when you enter (after she zips the flap), all you can hear are chirps. Not traffic. Not shouting. Not trains. And she plays Don McLean outside (at full volume), but you can't hear that from inside the tent, either, because there must be a million crickets, and the whole tent feels like some meadow off a gravel road way outside North Platte, Nebraska, and the only problem is them little suckers keep dying before she has the chance to replace them, and she's had to petition (successfully) the

Cerro Gordo County Tourism Bureau for help, which means, on any given day, maybe a third of the place is hers. Is volunteers collecting bugs. They bring them to her for inspection, and everyone who helps gets a free T-shirt, bright pink, and Buddy Holly's on it, and behind him are actual crickets (though one volunteer (a crusty old man from Mason City) once told her they looked more like grasshoppers, and the consensus was he was right but who else would notice, and changing it wasn't worth the cost of a second printing). Sometimes a protester or three will show up, and there will be arguments about animal cruelty and ecology and the relative value of arthropods or mollusks or chordates, and once a whole chain of folks drove over from the PETA chapter in Lincoln and shut down picking for a few hours. Random tourists got caught in the middle. Some of them took pictures, and most of those photos show people with signs and people with jars, and they're all mostly just staring at each other, though one picture (which happened to go viral) shows a man (who's bald and wears a beard and has these massive, four-inch holes in his ears) on his knees and half-surrounded by dust (and you can see the makeshift guitar memorial in the background), and he's holding a cricket up to his mouth like he's about to swallow it whole. You can practically hear it. Pretty much everyone is looking on in horror (albeit for different reasons), but it's also clear that nobody's planning to stop him. There are people who think someday the print will show up at the Art Institute of Chicago (right next to that famous Grant Wood), and maybe it will fill everyone who sees it with a kind of nostalgia, a fondness for big, empty spaces, for homespun shrines and undeveloped land, and some of the folks down at the Hy-Vee (and also the Fareway) think that this one picture (or maybe the soul of the cricket it shows) might be enough to save the site from the inevitable commercialization. The advance of progress. The building of a hotel or waterpark or convention center, and maybe it will make people want to be surrounded by ghosts. Maybe (though most of us know this is pretty much just wishful thinking) they'll want to hear nature. Chirping and mating calls and wind running through the backroads instead of elevators. Air conditioning. Waterslides and ice machines and flip-flops and all them dead echoes of the Great American Vacation.

Ritchie Valens

Almost Nearly Brothers

I leave Carlie Mae all high and dry right around Labor Day. Dale calls me five weeks later. He says the wife keeps giving him hell. Mostly on account of me, and Carlie Mae's lost 15 pounds and looks awfully good after three beers and even under a parka, and maybe now's the time to come crawling on back. I can tell he's at a ballfield. Probably out past the interstate. There's this hum of traffic in the background, and his mouth must be stuffed with chaw, and every so often a fence rattles like mad.

"Sisters," I say. "Have that vengeful loyalty."

"Guess so," he tells me, and then he fires another one toward the backstop. I can hear it pop. There's nothing for a while after that, just static and owls and wind ripping through the receiver, and then he says he forgives me, and I nod in this way I think he can hear. Anyway, he says, we'll get good and hammered when this blows over and somehow find a way to swerve ourselves on home.

"It won't," I say, "but we'll get together, anyhow," and then it's his turn to nod. To throw them dead hanging curveballs to no one on a wasted Cerro Gordo County night.

Five-Cent Redemption

Palacios used to drive this rusted-out Taurus through the alleys, and I'd get out and grab cans and bottles from people's recycling. Mostly it was cans. Usually beer. Sometimes the top layer would be all broken glass, and once I found dog shit or raccoon shit or human shit, and we thought maybe the guy heard us the last time and wanted to get a little revenge. That day was hot. Humid enough to fuck up your vision. Palacios and I had our shirts off, and he handed me a box of those Clorox wipes and started cracking jokes about women he never got to screw. He put his hand on my shoulder. It felt like gravel after a tornado, or else some kind of massive Iowa rain. I don't know why, but I was laughing my ass off and pretending to touch the steering wheel, to wipe shit all over the front seat. He said if I ever wanted to get hitched, the thing to do was hide the ring in one of these bins on this block right here. Get it down deep, he said. Get it down real good. And then she'll start digging, and maybe she'll be committed, or maybe you'll have half a chance when you decide you want to change your mind.

Nowhere Fast

Before my daughter Holly was born, I used to meet this woman out at the AmericInn, and afterward I'd get a lawn chair from the trunk. I'd head out to the interstate. I'd set up in the median and drink bottles of Coors for, like, an hour. Sometimes it would be just before lunch, and semis would rattle on by with pigs in the back, and I'd figure they were headed up to Hormel and then get queasy and starving all at once. Other times, it would be dead quiet. The middle of the night. I'd stare out at the airport. Think about driving away. About Wichita or Waco or Dallas, and one time, it was all moonless and humid, and I was imagining dancing La Bamba in 1959 when, just like that, there was nothing but headlights. An engine. I watched this midsize swerve off the road and hit some No U-Turn sign, and I swear I didn't dive for cover, just sat there stoic and drinking. Pretty sure the airbag deployed. The driver got out real slow. From the look of him, I knew he was running from something, and he started to wave at me like I was some deadbeat angel or a kindred spirit, and it didn't take half a second before I said fuck it. Fuck him. I threw an empty bottle toward his car. I turned tail and ran. He slurred some kind of empty curse, and the cops were probably on their way, and the last thing I heard was the car alarm. Or I guess it could have been the sound of busted glass.

Lighthouse Inn #4

Pederson likes to lean a tape recorder against the wall (which he knows is paper thin (and maybe that's why he's there in the first place)) and capture whatever's happening over in #6. Sometimes (or, well, rarely) it's sex noises. Crying. The voice of Alex Trebek. Once, there was a conversation about Buddy Holly and interstates, and (later, after it was archived) Pederson cranked the volume and held the recorder up to the microphone on his phone (something he does periodically) so that it would hear everything. So that it could take proper note. He Google searches things like arson. XKeyscore. He wants (the same way others want money or chocolate or Scarlett Johansson) to become interesting. To be a genuine "person of interest" (at least, as defined by the NSA). At night, he drives himself over to Mason City. Out to Waverly. Sometimes as far as Waterloo (and once even Apple Valley), and he scopes random Wi-Fi networks and downloads reams of (rural-themed) pornography, or he performs these deep-dive searches for homemade explosives and then goes and buys a dozen bags of fertilizer at Walmart (or (if they're open) Theisen's, or else the old Farm 'n' Seed), and he always pays by Visa, but then he leaves the bags out behind the store. He never takes them home (either because it's all a game, or maybe it's just that he doesn't have the space), and en route he calls an assortment of numbers (both residential and commercial) and figures the metadata will show him the whole way up and down 35, on Highway 20 or 18, and he leaves messages (including one at the headquarters for Royal Treatment Properties (a development group up in Minneapolis)) that end with the word "cipher" and invoke 9/11 and 7-Eleven and Islamic holidays all around. In the car, the music is classical (or sometimes it's rap (or else the kind of country that tells stories, or maybe the kind that feels like a Mad Lib)), and then, when he gets back to the motel, he watches documentaries on Timothy McVeigh and Ruby Ridge (and he even spent a week in Villisca once in 2018 (making sure to read up on the ax murders and then taking a million pictures of Randy Weaver's original home)) and waits for someone to knock on the door. Waits for the phone to ring. He asks the girl at the desk (who's 22 but looks 45) to keep an eye out for "G-men" (as if she has any clue) and mostly just lies on the bedspread. He listens to the whirring of the recorder. He masturbates and thinks about life (and death) and celebrity, and figures one of these days. One of these days, he'll be famous (and maybe it'll be because he finally decides to blow up that fancy new complex they're building out at the crash site (or maybe it'll be because he dies right there in #4 and then turns into (another) one of them haunted local legends (or maybe it'll be because it's 2159, and the lives of everyone (meaning their photos, their faces, their records of access and viewing habits and preferences, etc.) born after about 1970 are all (at least mostly) digitally archived and organized and displayed in museums (or else in some kind of massive electronic repository, some kind of human genome for lived experience), and his will be the wildest, the most goddamn fucking unique and artistic and interesting (though it never occurs to him that maybe thousands of others are trying the exact same thing)))), and what will the world say then, huh? Just think about who's the genius then.

Winter Dance Party

I never kissed another man, but I danced for one once, at this party in Cedar Falls, or I guess it could have been Waterloo. Everyone was dressed like dead rock stars, Waylon and Elvis and Tom Petty and the like. I went as Ritchie Valens, and this guy who said he knew my cousin Gregory told me I looked just like Lou Diamond Phillips. He said he'd pay me 84 dollars to stand in the corner and take my clothes off, and we'd somehow wandered upstairs. Techno was leaking from an unfinished basement. The whole place had thin carpet and smelled like a McDonald's.

"Okay," I said, and he promised not to touch himself. From the look of him, I figured he wouldn't try to touch me, either.

The blazer came first. Then the tie. I threw them both at his feet and added a little flair. Some hip movement, some eye contact, but all I got was this sense like he wanted me to get on with the show. So, I did. It got businesslike after a while. Like I was home alone and getting ready to take a shower. The last thing to go were the socks, and I was standing on a cigarette burn, and I swear I could feel the ash through what must have been three decades. Four, maybe. Or five. Five decades of ash on that carpet. He looked nervous. I think he said thank you. Then it turned out that all he had was two twenties and 17 ones, and "I'm sorry," he said, but I didn't care, and I drove home and told my roommates the whole night was wild. I said I'd found two girls, and both of them were eager, that my roommates should've fucking been there, man. They really fucking should've. I remember they got all wide-eyed and impressed, and I slept like a baby, or maybe I dreamt about the Surf Ballroom and the way it echoes on Saturday mornings before the tourists come, and I kept waking up every hour, it felt like, 2, 3, 4, and by 5 a.m. it hit me that none of this really happened. It was some kind of flashback or vision. I'd somehow managed to invent the whole miserable thing.

Do No Harm

There's this kid. College kid. Nineteen or 20, something like that, and nobody knows how many years exactly, but the bottom line is he can't drink. Not legally, anyway, though you can bet he's tossed a few back now and then, and it's these cans of Pabst he likes to drain in four big gulps and then throw way out into the Missouri River, or maybe it's the Cedar on account of they say he goes to UNI, and what does it matter, anyway, seeing as they both end up in the same place. Maybe it's one of these nights he comes up with the idea, all cold and wasted, on some dock or near an old railyard or abandoned slaughterhouse, or maybe it's at one of them winter dance parties they have once a year just off campus, and everyone's dressed like dead rock stars, and he wants to go as Jimi Hendrix but then picks Jim Morrison at the last minute instead and spends the whole night leaning up against a wall in some moldy basement. People are playing flip cup. Listening to EDM. And he's sitting there rocking back and forth and probably pretty fucked up, and all of a sudden, he's thinking, like, no way in hell do I want to have kids. Not now. Not ever. And who knows where this comes from, and it's probably one of them serotonin rushes or déjà vu, past-life flashbacks, and he doesn't do anything about it right then because, well, what can he do, but the point is that the idea sticks. Starts showing up in his dreams. Symbolically, of course. With the teeth falling out and the lizards carrying off his member and then feeding it to some snake lets you watch it bulge the whole way down, and there's all sorts of crazy shit like that, and so that summer he finds a urologist back home in Sioux City. Says he wants a vasectomy. The old snip, snip, snipperoni-roo, and the nurse gives him the evil eye. Scoffs out loud in his face, and he tries to tell her he's 35 and blessed with one of them baby faces, but, of course, she can see the goddamn chart, and there's the DOB right there, and she tells him the doc'll be in shortly and then slams the door on her way out, which doesn't bother him too much. Not really. He figures she's just jealous is what she is, and the doc doesn't look much older than him, and they talk about football and Russell Crowe, and it's real nice until the guy says, sorry, son, I can't fucking do it, and so, wait, says the kid. What do you mean? And the doctor tells him this whole story is just made for local media, and he don't trust his nurse, and this place is one of them early-career postings, you understand, and that goes for journalists, too, and this is fucking catnip, kid. It's clickbait. Because this here's Woodbury County. This here's the Iowa 4th. And just what kind of meal do you think they'll make out of some doc fresh from Iowa City, and maybe the second thing he does is sterilize some teenager, some juvenile, they'll say, and we know the truth, and you're within your rights, and maybe at this point the doc says that he actually wishes he had the convictions of this kid, but that don't change the facts and the hassle. The risk. It's just too much, he says, and this is where I got to draw the line.

The kid don't take too kindly to this, of course, but what's he gonna do? Hire a lawyer? And he don't have the first clue how that would look or where he'd even go, and so he does what anyone his age would and goes home and writes up some social media diatribe and drinks himself to sleep, and by the next morning the feed's gone crazy. Haywire. It's trending nationally, and maybe two days later, whole busloads of protestors are already coming in from 80 or 90 and up or down 29, depending, and then there's U.S. 75 and 20, too, and these folks, they come in all different kinds of stripes, and some of them are calling the kid an environmental hero, and others are all about men's rights, and they got signs that say "Guy's body, Guy's choice," and some of these guys are named Guy, and, years later, one of them will write this deeply philosophical manifesto about the history of women withholding sex in order to maintain or reverse relational power dynamics, and this kid here was just the ticket, he'll write, was a figure of damn near religious significance, and whole armies of young men getting secret vasectomies is the only way to take back control, the only way to restore the patriarchy, and the whole thing will feel florid and alive despite being functionally incoherent, and the end result will be that this little treatise becomes both an underground bestseller and also the symbolic representation of a certain strain of taboo politics, and all that isn't even mentioning the evangelicals, who show up at this kid's door first and with these real committed faces talking up how every potential life is a little piece of God's miracle work, and a whole host of them don't even have to drive too far, neither, and the Catholics get there pretty fucking soon after, practically right on their heels, and they're even more militant, and that means there's news trucks outside this kid's window by day-three noon, and they ain't from KTIV, that's for sure. They got big red letters on 'em. Fancy cameras. The reporters got on these tight skirts and Italian blazers, and this kid's parents are telling him he's got to go out there and make some kind of statement, got to get the whole thing under control somehow, and so he steps out onto his front lawn wearing some Golden Gophers bathrobe used to belong to his old man back in his undergrad days, and the thing's loud enough to wake the dead, assuming the media trucks and the protestors haven't rattled them up already, and he says this decision ain't got nothing to do with politics, and what it is is all personal and private, and I never intended to start no big to-do, and, oh, of course that shuts everyone right up, doesn't it? Really shames the fuckers. Especially when the kid does in fact have one of them freshly telegenic baby faces and those wide-set eyes that are all-fire kind and innocent, and he's an absolute ratings monster, isn't he, and these women start writing him letters that are, like, real, real suggestive, and all sorts of young men everywhere are saying he's a revolutionary, a goddamn inspiration, and they're sending photos of themselves just after their own vasectomies, and these kids are younger than him, even, and people start getting the procedure on their 18th birthdays, and the whole thing becomes its own little ritual in New York and Vancouver and London, and it gets everywhere. It goes fucking global. He's this prairie farm-town celebrity, and the only problem is he still can't find a provider, still can't get one himself, or, then again, maybe he can, and there are offers coming in all the time, and some of them are even sending contracts and saying they'll pay him, that they'll put him on TV as some kind of square-jawed messiah for modern men's health, except the problem is that now he ain't even sure he wants it. It was supposed to be about breaking the mold, and now it'll only look crass and/or commercial, and maybe the truth is that the really rebellious thing would be to become functionally celibate, at least as far as other people are concerned, and just to spill all them little packets of DNA down toilet pipes and into tube socks and tissues in some velvet basement stocked with a 3D, virtual-reality Blu-ray player just especially made for projecting curvy, bouncing women with names like Laramie and Cheyenne onto this real high-end OLED monitor, and yeah, he figures, that's the next natural step. That's what he really wants. And for a second he feels a little sad or almost guilty because there's this creeping realization like this is something he probably should've known from the first. Something he wishes he'd understood all along.

Sanctuary City

Palacios lived in a church for a month. It was Saint Barbara's. Locust Street. The night of his 35th birthday, me and Fillmore climbed through the basement window. We brought Grain Belt and donuts and a dirty magazine we had to stop at six places to find, and for a while we thought they didn't even sell dirty mags anymore. The centerfold was dark and green-eyed, and she reminded us of dirt roads and ranchland and places with no lights. Places you could really see the sky.

"Shit," said Palacios. "It's been a fucking year," and we nodded. There wasn't anything else to say.

For a while we drank in the mothers' chapel. It smelled like diapers and cheap perfume, and we lit a few cigarettes to try and cover it up. At some point, Fillmore asked about the smoke detector, and Palacios said he raided them batteries ages ago, and the boredom was one crusty motherfucker, but if we really wanted to party, he knew where Father Barrett kept the hard stuff. The collection plate and the old communion wafers and some other shit you'd be shocked to find, and so we followed him back toward the sacristy. It was cold. Fillmore kept throwing the flashlight up to stained glass, and for some reason one of the windows had a picture of soldiers stacking cannonballs, and we guessed it was donated by the VFW, or maybe the Knights of Columbus. Palacios went behind the altar. We heard metal scraping. I said it was like being an altar boy all over again, only with a cheaper kind of thrill, and

Palacios came out with tight fists. With a few crumpled fives in his left. Shaking some pills in his right. Fillmore said, "That's what I'm talking about," and I kept looking up at the crucifix. At the blood on the ribcage. The nails in the hands. I saw Palacios coming toward us and then put out my palm and thought how Jesus was dead. Jesus was a man. I figured He'd probably forgive whatever we were about to do.

Narratology

The story's been going around forever, but it always peaks after prelims, and there are whispers in the bookstores and signs on the quad, and the grad students discourse in the bars along Dubuque Street, and the main character is always a woman. Her name is Lacy. Lucy. Lynelle. She's ABD and three days from defending (having spent the last two years floating from river to river in search of a kind of flood myth, a story she thinks they tell all over Iowa (with small variations), and it's about a bowler who honed his (or (in one case that she's been able to document) her) craft in local alleys and read wax patterns and spin trajectories and drank and talked shit and lost bets and then nearly (or actually) made it big (and won tournaments and hustled old pros and generally lived the life of Riley)) and getting blowback from advisors and friends and even the outside committee member, and they're threatening major revision (or outright rejection) and the cutting of funds, and what it boils down to is a lack of documentation, an inability to find any formalized, written evidence for what she's labeled (in a fit of punch-drunk exhaustion after eating a batch of chocolate laced with THC) the Bowl-Ur Myth, and all she's got are oral interviews, and most of the subjects (including a man from Cedar Rapids who said he was born in Grinnell but for whom no official records exist) are refusing to respond to university correspondence. The name Stephen Glass is getting thrown around. Jayson Blair. And this Lacy swears to Christ she's got every word on tape, only there's video all over her social media, and it's got her doing impressions. Good ones. All kinds of celebrities (including John Mellencamp and John Cusack and John Prine) and also invented characters. Sketches of people who sound like Midwesterners, like residents of Lake Wobegon, and her advisor (they say on the strength of an anonymous tip from another grad student (a former lover, says one version (while still another calls him a stalker (or, variously, a frat boy, a football player, a flunked former student)))) feeds transcripts of these impressions and her submitted recordings into an algorithm borrowed from the folks over in Linguistics, and what comes out is an argot the program labels 97 percent similar, and so there's talk of probation. Suspension. Even the mention of a little-used (to the point that longtime tenured faculty swore it was a myth) blacklist that essentially disqualifies members from any tenure-line job anywhere in the respectable world (leaving open only the potential for adjunct gigs at for-profits and summers teaching English in, say, Namibia (or maybe fallout-drenched New Mexico)), and that's where the momentum is, they say. That's where Lucy's going to end up. Which she, of course, gets wind of (and usually it's through some famous writer teaching at the Workshop (through Toni Morrison or Margaret Atwood or John Updike (coming through on the lecture circuit, and he finds her in the corner at some post-reading party and tips a beer and looks her dead in the eye and says (maybe with a hand on her elbow), "Run, Rabbit"), and once it was Thomas Pynchon (or, at least, a guy who said he was Pynchon (or someone who "communed" with Pynchon))), or else via anonymous note (though frequently one submitted by a friend of a friend of a friend of whoever happens to be narrating this particular version of the story)), and it takes her two days to pack, and the morning of the official defense (or sometimes of an emergency meeting scheduled in lieu of the formal defense), she's just gone. Left town. Empty office (or maybe she leaves behind a cryptic note (a "fuck you" carved into a metal desk they end up having to move into basement storage (and you can find it, they say, if you talk to the right custodian, if you grease a few palms or just know where to look))) and empty apartment and hopped a train to Fort Dodge, as they say, and the whole committee and perhaps a third of her cohort and maybe 10 random passersby (including (sometimes) an elderly man who has not missed either a Hawkeyes home game or sports-related dissertation defense since 1972) are left chewing on rubber bagels and tapping their feet while the committee whispers about sanctions and whether it's worth filing the paper-work (and here there's usually a joke about how the audi-ence clearly knows what's coming next), and, turns out (surprise, surprise), it's not, and so they never do. And Lynelle's still ABD. In good standing. And nobody knows where she is, but she's out there somewhere (or maybe she jumped into the Iowa River (or is (right this very instant) drinking Coors Light and working on a Dutch 200 at La Bamba Bowl in Clear Lake (or grinding away on the PWBA tour (or even training for the U.S. Bowling Open in Reno (or Syracuse (or Baton Rouge (or Tulsa)))))))), and (the narrator says to whichever strung-out dissertator is within weeks of presenting) in that you should take comfort. Say a prayer to Saint Lacy, and maybe she'll get you through, and some folks do, and others don't, and still others think the whole story is a scam, a camp thing, a rite of initiation, a kind of exquisite-corpse pyramid scheme invented to make the next year's cohort feel even more obsessive or maybe inferior (and they say somebody once (ironically?) submitted a doctoral prospectus proposing a Foucauldian analysis of the Lucy story itself), and as we speak, there are students doing graffiti on the bridge back behind the Old Capitol. "Lynelle doesn't exist," it says. And, "Lacy wasn't here." And below that, someone's written (in smaller print) "Neither were you." And below that, it says (even smaller (as in, you can barely see)) "Neither was I." And soon the college cops will find it, and they'll call in maintenance, and maintenance will hire some painters, and maybe they'll be professional, or they could be teenagers on community service, and, either way, they'll do a good job, and it'll look nearly brand new, but if you've got good eyes (and you know where to direct them), what you'll see is one last line. And who knows who wrote it (and I swear it's not me), but the thing that it says is neither was anything, really. Or, to put it more exactly, what it actually says is, in point of fact: "Neither was any of this."

Food Court

It smelled like Sbarro and wishing wells, and Holly and I watched a man fall down the escalator. He was at a dead sprint with these two overweight security guards on his tail, and then he yelled something, then one of his shoes caught, and the rest was gasping and clanging and whirring and fluorescence. Some people laughed. A few didn't look up from their phones. Holly said, "Let's get a look before they haul him away" because she wanted to see if he was still conscious, if what he yelled was really her name.

Amish Bakery

There was one maybe 90 miles away, and I took Carlie Mae on a Saturday because she was still acting real depressed. The baker said his name was Malachi. He had green eyes. Clean shave. Shoulders wide as a doorway, and he looked at us like we were Jesus Christ come again, so we bought more cinnamon rolls than Dale's whole family could eat, enough bread for an army of ducks.

Carlie Mae did that thing where she leans forward all direct and thinks she's being coy. "All these loaves," she said. "You got a couple of fishes back there, too?"

"Careful there, ma'am. You're bordering on blasphemy." Malachi wasn't smiling, but underneath you could tell he kind of was. She didn't talk about it, but I knew Carlie Mae was replaying every last detail the whole rest of the trip, and it was something in the way she stuck her hand out the window and rolled it in the wind like just-so, and who could blame her? I'd've probably done the same damn thing.

When we got back home, Dale was on the couch watching the Hawkeyes. They must've been losing because he didn't even say hello or nothing. Just eyes locked dead on the screen, and all we got was, "You know those assholes ain't even Amish, right? It's an act, darlin'. Something they do for money. Make you think you're supporting some noble cause, and then they're out all night drinking and chasing tail just like anyone else."

"What do you know about it?" said Carlie Mae, and I

don't know if it was for her sake or mine, but for once I did not fight him. I just stared out the window. Watched these massive clouds roll in from the west and prayed to every god I could think of to—Please. If you can spare it.—let my jackass of a husband maybe, finally, somehow be just a little bit right.

Revelation

On Saturdays, men would come to our house in dress shirts and ties, and they'd give us bibles and magazines, and Dad and Uncle Bernie would be passed out or hiding in the basement, and so my brother would offer the men lemonade spiked with Karkov because he wanted to bring them low, to show them real family hospitality, and he said they were Mormons, or maybe Jehovah's Witnesses, and most of the time the men would either decline or else take a polite sip and then slide the glass away all ginger, like it was a snapping turtle or some kind of deadly frog, but one guy, I remember, he slammed the whole thing, and he was tall and sounded like Buck Owens, and we tried not to look at him while he dropped two brochures on the table, then spent 20 minutes talking about these camps they had, these barns on open acreage and all up and down the Missouri River, and they were for kids like us, he said, for searchers, for outcasts, and if we ever got up the courage, we should move ourselves out there just as fast as we could because he swore on his mission we'd come out reborn, bathed in the spirit and plumb full of life and zest and brand shining new, and my brother nodded and told him we had to get over to the Fareway, even though we still had half a pizza sitting in the fridge, and then the man left with these footsteps so quiet it was like he was never there at all, and the next Saturday my brother pinned a centerfold to the door, this woman he always talked about, and she went by different names, but it was Laramie back then, and he said she was a talisman, some kind of charm or spell to ward the guy off just in case he was thinking of coming back. Something seemed wrong with my brother for weeks after that, but I didn't really understand what it was until I turned 16 and took the Silverado out to find these camps myself, and it was Highway 20 to Sioux City and then south all aimless on I-29, and there was nothing but broken-down barns and farmland and crosses and roadkill, and some of the barns had religious messages painted on them, things like "Get Right" or "Repent" or "Protect Life," but mostly everything was deserted and empty, and I thought it looked like pictures from World War II. It didn't hit me until I was driving back that this whole place was a threat, that whatever god there was, he skipped town a long time ago.

Summer Dance Party

Must have been around last July or so, and me and McQuaid crash this party over in Clear Lake. Bunch of college kids. Everyone's dressed like dead celebrities. Elvis is there. Tom Petty, too. John Wayne looks all clean and like a banker in training, and we get him dosed up real good on this corn mash we sometimes make in my garage, and by the time 11 o'clock rolls around, the asshole can barely walk. Can hardly stand up. So, we get him in the back of the truck, and he's puking practically the whole way out to this cornfield back behind some dentist office McQuaid went to as a kid, and nobody's there. Place is fucking deserted. It's gotta be 90 degrees even though it's past midnight, and the bugs are going crazy around the headlights, and we drag him out of the parking lot and plant him a few rows deep. We put his cowboy hat over his face. Cover him up with dirt. We stick a couple ears down his pants and toss one up by his teeth in case he gets hungry, and then when he's passed out just real clear and good, McQuaid grabs the guy's shoes and socks, and we hightail it back to the interstate. Just lit out straight for home. We figure if he's got any little bit of Duke in him at all, then he'll make out fine, and, wouldn't you know it, that's exactly what he does. We hear about it sometime later. Who knows if it's true. But what happens is some hygienist finds him the next morning, and she says he must have about 150 mosquito bites and is red and scratched and flaking pretty much all up and down everywhere, and she wants to call the cops, but he shrugs her off, then gets a ride home from some old high school buddy. Or his stepdad. Point is, he's all right and no harm done, and me and McQuaid still see him around town sometimes, at Buddy's over in Mason City, or else at the Fareway, and word is he dropped out of school. Came back home. He doesn't recognize us, I don't think, or at least he never acts like he does, and me and McQuaid wouldn't give two shits, anyway, but we do get real silent for a minute or so when he walks by, just as sort of, like, a tribute, and then we go back to buying liquor. Start talking about football.

"Vikes are really gonna fuck up that Rodgers on Sunday, ain't they?" he'll say, and I'll nod. We'll laugh. Bottles will rattle around and echo from somewhere, and damn right, I'll say, even though we both know it'll be the same story all over again, and he'll probably carve up our defense real good. Carve us like we're pumpkins. Or else one of them big old Christmas hams.

Lover of Mankind

At Uncle Bernie's funeral we went all high-end and stocked the bar with Jack Daniel's and Johnnie Walker and then hired waiters to wear tuxedos and come around with them bacon-wrapped scallops and lobster tails and filets, and, sure, there wasn't no estate and not much life insurance, either, but we rented out the Surf anyway and maxed out six credit cards and chased top shelf with Heineken, and we even paid a Bernie Sanders impersonator to give the eulogy, and he talked about railroads and lunch pails and brotherhood and said, from one Bernie to another, and we raised our glasses and promised to eat until we yakked, to clog our own arteries in solidarity, and we laid the casket out on the stage, and it was right where Buddy Holly would have stood, and then we danced and fell and invited the whole town in with us, just anyone passing by on the street, and some of them were girls, and Dad and my brother tried to bring them home, but Dad kept getting choked up, and my brother kept leering at their chests and sometimes their legs, and so we all stumbled out through the doors alone and into February, and it was maybe 12 below, and our ears were cold, but our guts were warm, and my brother said we'd be in debt forever, and we said hell yeah, and fuck it, and the bill collectors could call and call and call and we wouldn't answer, or, if we did, we'd tell them to eat tar and choke on exhaust, and then we'd make them file a shitload of paperwork in order to get anything, and maybe we'd be dead before any of it came through, or, even if we weren't, even if they garnished our wages, who really cared because we knew there'd be enough left for Wi-Fi and High Life and scratchers, and if Uncle Bernie knew anything, it was those were the things that really mattered, and wasn't it everything a man could ever need.

New Colossus

We hoped it was Ecstasy, but it was probably Adderall, or maybe even Wellbutrin, and Fillmore and I sat in the pews waiting for it to kick in. Palacios lit candles. He didn't put any money in the slot. Just grabbed the stick and torched them one by one, and Fillmore cursed and pretended it was a prayer. We had a Wiffle ball with us and one of them plastic yellow bats. We stood under the balcony in the back and took wild swings and tried to call our shots. Aimed for the Stations of the Cross. Jesus falls the first time. Veronica wipes His face. Palacios took a turn and smacked one all the way up to the altar, and it clanged off Jesus' ribs, and Palacios went sprinting around the church like the Indians had won the World Series, and I found the ball and checked it for blood, but there wasn't any. It still looked brand shining new. Then, Palacios slid into home, and the whole place echoed, and he said in six months it would be caucus time, and everyone would be traipsing around the state, shaking hands and making deals, and he'd still be stuck here or possibly deported already, maybe in holding somewhere in Illinois or Nebraska, and he used to love seeing all them bumper stickers in the parking lot at the Fareway, and he asked Fillmore and me if we'd scratch a few off for him or else maybe just grab a couple ourselves. None in particular. This wasn't political. What it was was he liked the colors and the block letters, and we could mail them in bright white envelopes with Teddy Roosevelt stamps. We could bring them to the church if Palacios was still there, and me and Fillmore stared at the tile. I told him, I said, sure, why not, and we'll send you the whole array, and he could consider it a promise, but all Palacios did was nod. Was walk back over to the candles. He licked his fingers and snuffed the flames. I couldn't see his face, but his shoulders looked focused and sure, and I figured he must have got the message, must have known what it was that I meant.

Hail to the Chief

When Frank Dent died (unexpectedly (sometime in the early-2020s)), his daughter turned about a hundred documents (taken from the hard drive of his home computer (an old HP desktop he'd had since 2004 (and (it was rumored) used mainly for downloading pornography))) over to the DNC for what she called "evaluation and inspiration." Among other things, these documents contained: (essentially meaningless) philosophical musings about the future of humanity (including the assertion that human beings circa 2159 would talk about modern humanity's willingness to drive cars the way modern humanity talks about 18th- (and 19th- (and, really, 3rd- and 4th- and 17th- (and c.))) century humanity's desire to own slaves (meaning as a kind of totalizing black mark on just about everyone alive at the time)), effusive praise of parliamentary democracy, attacks against the First Amendment, and radical ideas about the historical progression of American elections, one of which involved a 200-page treatise (or, as some called it, a "deranged rant") on the electoral potential of artificial-intelligence programs that could be designed for the express purpose of running for office (and then (once elected (presumably after either a Constitutional amendment or (insanely) friendly judicial decision regarding Article II, Section 1, Clause 5)) hooked up to a kind of permanent workstation in the Oval Office, where it (meaning the program (or, the president, as it were)) could be fed information from the CIA, the NSA, the DoD, the BLM, the CBO, the GAO, and pretty much any properly digitized (which meant pretty much any, really) U.S. government department and/or agency for the explicit purpose of designing legislation, crafting economic policy, making military determinations, etc., and the beauty of this was the removal of emotion (even if (as Dent acknowledged) secondary programs might (and probably would) have to be designed (on account of traditional speechwriters would likely no longer be trusted) in order to give cohesive, impactful rhetorical summaries (read: speeches) that justified or explained presidential actions), the (drastic) diminishing of electoral considerations (though the treatise (which utilized footnotes and endnotes, as well as reams of interlocking parentheticals) made allowances for the fact that, yes, said programs could be designed to prioritize (even to the exclusion of all else) political strategy, whether during debates or on the stump or what have you (though Dent argued that this kind of coding would ultimately produce hollow, inauthentic answers, and the voting public would reject such blatantly calculated responses in favor of the more direct, straightforward, and policy-specific answers that would be shared by a "more rationally" crafted program, citing the American people's blatant hunger for politicians who refused the "dark arts" of focus groups and question-dodging and spin)), and the idea that, finally (meaning once this idea of his became reality), the random, poll- and media-driven narratives about electoral viability and the quadrennial dance through various "Midwestern nowheres" (which, Dent made clear, being from Nebraska (and having spent years of his life at roadside Iowa motels and feedlots and coffee shops), he loved and toward which he meant no disrespect) would be meaningless, would cease to infiltrate our collective consciousness, and, for once, we could vote for what we actually want, which is the best-designed leader, the leader with the best judgment, the best internal priorities, and (even if there were the obvious risk of cyberattack, and, of course, various operating system security protocols and network maintenance techniques would have to be part of the broader discussion) may the best design team win), and this was the one that wound up leaking to the media. It didn't cause hysteria, per se. More like fevered amusement, and there were memes about *Terminator* and *The Artificial President* (as written by Aaron Sorkin), and the crew of *Meet the Press* spent the last five minutes of their panel discussion laughing about the whole concept. They talked about moral panics. About cars and social networks and mobile devices and brain cancer, and Hugh Hewitt got real (or maybe faux) serious and said all forms of technology were inherently (and radically) liberal, while a (female) columnist from the *Washington Post* looked on in disgust and then ended the show by saying this: "It figures. Because what a joke. And this is the future, and this is the truth, and the truth is the American people would rather be ruled by a computer than a human woman, and shouldn't that tell you everything you need to know?"

Spin It Straight, Spin It True

So, there's this senator running for reelection out of Iowa or Kansas or wherever, and he's got us on retainer, and lucky for him, too, because sometime in late September, his browser history gets hacked by this oddball group of radical feminists and old Jerry Falwell acolytes, and turns out this guy's got a thing for porn. Nothing serious, mind you. A few videos a month. Maybe one every two weeks, and they always involve this gal named Laramie Voyeur, and none of them are even real kinky or nothing, just your run-of-the-mill porno shit. You know, like they got her dressed as a cheerleader. A nurse. An office worker. In one of them, she's playing the farmer's daughter type, and that one the senator apparently watched seven or eight times, and there are theories about whether he was studying it for electoral clues or else just trying to make it through without coming, and in the meantime CNN's bringing on these Dr. Ruth copycats who spend minutes at a time talking about psychosexual development processes while the anchors nod soberly and then throw it to a panel for an argument over depravity and Christian values and the relevance of personal sexual behavior to fitness for public office. Some people start talking about this senator as a kind of cult hero. Others call him a perv and make Lewinsky jokes, and this meme goes around about him conducting staff interviews at Hooters and then looking reporters up and down with them elevator eyes as the reporters ask him questions. This is all before any official response is crafted for the public, mind you, and so the senator's staff is up our asses. They want to know what to say and how to frame it, and his campaign chair suggests this kind of "he who is without sin" angle and gives us this packet of, like, sociological surveys that highlight masturbatory trends and single, adult male habits, and the whole idea is to paint his candidate as essentially boring, mainly. As typical. And, of course, fully capable of understanding the staged nature of pornography, that it's "the functional equivalent of comparing, like, you know, a *Batman* movie to the actual experience of being a New York police officer trying to fight crime every day, and maybe that will win us some of that cop support, right?" So, "No," we tell him. And everyone listening will lose you at sin, and what you got to do is embrace it. Own it. Your guy's got to go to the podium, and he's got to bring his wife, and together they got to look into a camera while he says the following. She's got her arm around his waist, mind you. She's looking put-together in some kind of blazer or sweater, and it's tight but professional, okay? Like, showing the senator has an appreciation for beauty without throwing its tits in our face, and what he says is this. He says, "There's no truth to those claims of responsibility you've been hearing, and the thing is I wasn't hacked. We put that shit out there." We're paraphrasing here, you understand. "We put that shit out there, and we wanted voters to see it, and I doubt my opponent will do the same, even though the American people deserve an honest conversation. They deserve the truth. And the truth is that I love my wife, and I love women, and sometimes there's nothing better than watching a beautiful, tanned performer twirling and moving all comfortable with her own sexuality. There's nothing better than watching two toned, consenting adults getting good and together and fucked, and at least I'm honest enough to tell you where I stand and let the voters make up their minds, and you won't hear that from my opponent, who [he subtly implies] is into way worse shit, shit that'll make your skin crawl," and the campaign man just looks at us. You can tell he thinks we're bonkers. Like, we got to be completely nuts. This is the Midwest, he's thinking. Salt of the Earth and down-home values and Good People, and they want my candidate to come out in favor of hardcore pornography starring a woman who looks like she's probably Mexican, and what could we tell him? That we had the data? That this was his best shot? What we ended up saying was double or nothing. Was, you go and do it right, and we'll take a hefty bonus if you win, but, if you lose, the whole campaign's worth of services is all on us, and would you believe that fucker didn't say yes in the room? He shook and shrugged and said he had to make some calls, but we all knew what he'd do just about immediately, and that's the beauty of this business, isn't it? Sound confident, and they will believe you. Tell them what's what, and they'll do anything you want.

Protected Class

Sometime later, my brother bought a cheap camper from this old gearhead out in Manly and fixed it up good. Drove it up to Minnesota. He parked it in some trailer yard outside the city and then smoked Winston Reds in the kitchen and let bananas go rancid on the counter. He ate beans from a can. Played his music too loud and sometimes ran after dogs that walked by, or else made these little shotgun motions with his hands, and that freaked the neighbors right out, but they said he always paid his lot rent, and mostly folks just left him alone, but then one night we get word the cops caught him in some cul-de-sac over in Eden Prairie, and they said he was spray-painting the hammer and sickle on people's doorsteps. Taping Ted Kaczynski excerpts to windshields and denting BMWs, and they say he did it real quiet and little by little, and the neighbors started getting scared and on edge and outing all each other's addictions and affairs and porno collections, and everyone agrees he could've got away with the whole thing real easy except he decided to stand naked and shouting in front of some lawyer's place, so they hauled him off to lockup and stuck him with the public defender. I don't remember how long the trial took. Somebody called him a mastermind, I think. They said the damage ran six figures, or maybe seven on account of property values was real high to begin with. At sentencing, the prosecutor asked the judge to go hard. To take into consideration the planning and the motivation, the real specific targeting, and for a while the prosecutor said she thought about charging terrorism, or at least a hate crime, and, when it was my brother's turn, he said he'd always had hate in his heart, and, if that made it a hate crime, then fine. So be it. Or, and this is what he asked the judge to consider, was that maybe they all had it coming. Maybe they finally understood how we felt.

Real American Prophets

Back when they built that new hotel out by the interstate, I'd drive up there a couple, three times a month and get a fresh room and then put the Book of Mormon in the dresser drawer, put it right there next to the Bible. I'd put my phone number in there, too. Along with a Buddy Holly postcard. I'd write, "Surf Ballroom Bliss" or "Nine Digits from Heaven," and I didn't know what any of that meant, but I liked how it sounded. I liked how it felt. And then I'd go down to the lobby and try to cancel the room, and maybe they'd do it, or maybe they wouldn't, and maybe I'd have to run up some credit, to stay and surf channels and listen to footsteps and vacuums and air conditioners, and either way, I'd eventually head back home and wait for the phone to ring. I'd wait for the static. For bad reception. For sand-baked voices telling me about Joseph Smith and the prophet Nephi and what to do to get ready for End Times, but the point is no one ever did. No one ever called. Then I went and I got this fancy new phone, and I had to change my number, and now all I can think is that somebody out there's trying right this instant, and all he's getting are them three broken beeps and that mechanical woman, and I'm thinking I missed my chance. Missed my calling. And I oughta just go back there with a stack of new postcards and nine fresh digits, but then I bet those books ain't even there. And nothing stays the same. And they clear out your shit faster than you can smile, and it's like how some people worry about children is you'll open the drawers, and they'll be empty and white, and here's the thing. Is the paint's so goddamn bright you can't even bear to look.

Great American Vacation

They build that hotel out on top of the old Buddy Holly crash site, and there's this big grand opening with a packed parking lot, and then, bam. Bed bugs. Everywhere. People find them all up and down the mattresses, and sometimes it's the live specimens, and other times it's those little waste trails the bugs leave behind, and the guests, they go straight to the front desk. They got the bugs folded up between sheets of hotel stationery. Inside Ziplocs sometimes. They strip naked and just abandon the clothes and the luggage, and the highways are crammed in all directions with bare asses on heated leather, and they drive back to Omaha and Minneapolis and Lubbock and Chicago, and the company that built the place, this Royal Treatment Properties up near that Mall of America, they know they're gonna spend the next year (at least) giving out reimbursements. Free passes. They can see the class action from a mile away, and God only knows what the settlement will cost, and, from the look of things, you'd think that would just about be the end of the story. Ol' Buddy gets the last laugh, and they knock the place down or repurpose it as some kind of something else, or they just end up unloading it for pennies on the dollar to some other Hospitality, Inc., so they can take their shot, but that isn't what happens. Not even close. Well, they do pay out impacted customers. Replace socks and suitcases and run these one-time, all-inclusive getaway specials good at any RTP property anywhere in the good old U. S. of A., and of course there's still that lawsuit hung up in litigation or what have you, but what happens next is some low-level marketing staffer files this memo that says: "Well, hey, why not leave the bugs alive? Not everywhere, mind you, but just in one room. And maybe it's the one right above that spot where they found the Big Bopper, and I know it was supposed to be the Honeymoon Suite, but let's repurpose the fucker, and I think we can get people to pay for the privilege. Like, sell them a night of haunted bloodsucking and old-time immersion," and this is a nutso idea, everyone says, but this marketing guy is connected somehow. He's somebody's nephew or third cousin or friend of a dear family friend, and so the whole idea gets passed up the chain as a courtesy and then kicked around departments for a while until somehow it lands on the desk of this guy Warren Hafner, and by this time the original bugs is long dead (having been fumigated and refumigated and choked into chemical dust), but he says fuck it. Let's give this thing a try. And Warren's got this kind of mad-scientist rep about him since they say he's the one invented reality tourism or something like that (not to mention he's been involved with the whole Buddy Holly project from the very beginning), and, so, people listen. They get these jars of bed bugs from an exterminator in Fridley, or could be it's Coon Rapids, and Hafner drives them down 35 himself (in this 2006 Toyota Corolla he just fucking loves because it makes him look inconspicuous; it makes him look like somebody's frugal mother) and opens the jars in what used to be the Honeymoon Suite, and he spearheads the establishment of all these elaborate precautions and protocols and gets some kind of greased-palm permission from the health department, and what it boils down to is this: Once guests enter the suite, they can't leave. And their clothes and personal belongings (there's a lockbox in the lobby for watches and cufflinks and purses and the like) have to stay behind. And they've all gotta take this decontamination shower at checkout (as if they're leaving (or entering, more like) a prison), and wouldn't you know it, people sign up. Artists, mostly. Sometimes newlyweds. Hipsters and rich city folk with time to spare and money to burn, and they all cite this desire, this outright fucking hunger for experience, man, and these people pay upward of 900 a night. Triple during the week of February 3rd, and something like 5K on the anniversary itself, and they stay up all night to feel every single bite. There's no TV in the room. Just this old record player, and it's playing Winter Dance Party Live, and they say somebody recorded it at the Surf that very night, but it's really probably from some other stop along the tour (or else not even authentic, at all), and these idiots dance on the bed. They screw on top of all them tiny little vampires, and sometimes they get blood on the sheets, and it doesn't matter one bit because the hotel just fucking tosses the bedding after each guest, anyway, and the rates more than cover it. They don't even have to advertise. The internet picks it up. Various alt weeklies. It gets named "Offbeat Vacation of the Year" in some big-shot, L.A. travel mag, and Hafner (who, by this time, has gone from behind-the-scenes cult figure to full-on hospitality celebrity), he's giving these big-appearance-fee lectures out at Cornell basically monthly, and every Trump hotel on the planet is calling Hafner constantly, and the crowds, they give him these roaring greetings and standing O's. They chant his name. Sometimes people give him dead (or living) bed bugs in shoeboxes or pressed between panes of glass, and the whole thing becomes this phenomenon. This sensation. Somebody even makes a documentary about the people that stay in this infested, corn-country room ("this B&B from hell," as the director called it), and there's all kinds of debate about whether it's one of them genuine docs or somehow just scripted real nice and subtle, and at the end of it, they zoom tight on the face of a writer who's working on a story cycle about Buddy Holly and Clear Lake, Iowa, and he's got these massive ears and big buck teeth, and he looks a little like Alfred E. Neuman (only a shade uglier), and they ask him, they go, what was it like, and do you feel inspired, and fuck, he says. Yeah. And I swear to Christ Almighty. Their beaks, he says. You can feel them way down past your caffeinated soul.

The Big Bopper

All Systems Go

Some nights, me and Fillmore would get good and sauced, then head on out to the interstate. He'd stand on the median, and I'd be over by the AmericInn, and we'd throw a football back and forth. We'd tiptoe the shoulder. Dodge traffic or run post patterns toward pylons that were really exit signs, and this one time we got the ball lodged inside a semi. It wasn't an accident. It was a goddamn miracle. The truck had those slats so the animals could breathe, and we laid face up in the ditch and talked about health codes. About what they'd do when they found it. He said they'd have to spike the whole shipment, and I said they'd just cut it up with the cattle, and for weeks after that, we'd buy ground round on discount down at the Fareway and check it for leather. For laces. And of course, nothing like that ever showed up, and then he quit drinking, and now I go out there all by myself. I lay in the grass. I look at the stars. The trucks still come by, and the axles still rattle, and I think how there's really no stopping them, and ain't that just the way it has to be.

Just Another Fish

My brother's wife leaves him for a pharmacist, and my bro goes a little apeshit. Buys this big tent from Scheels. Real heavy duty. He sets it up in the yard, and after a week, it smells like methane and cut grass and cigarettes, and the boys bring him Hamburger Helper and McDonald's for dinner, and one night he calls me and says to get my ass on over, and we play Wiffle ball. We talk about pills. We split a 12-pack, and then we drive out to the lake, and he tells me he's got a gun in his glove box, and it's this old .38 he bought on discount someplace downtown. He takes it out and shows me it's loaded. I put my hands up like, hey, man, back off. He's got dirt under his nails and generally looks like shit, and I follow him down to the edge of the dock where we stare at shadows. At this red October moon. He throws the gun into the night, and we stand there watching it spin like a boomerang, and I see him jump in and stay underwater for 10 seconds, or maybe something more like 12.

When he comes up, he climbs onto the dock and sits there shivering. I punch him in the shoulder. I tell him he looks like a drowned rat. I say, well, she sure ain't coming back now, is she, and he just looks at me, and after a couple of coughs, we start laughing harder than we have in months. Years. As long as I can remember, and maybe our whole damn lives.

Lighthouse Inn #1

They say it happens every year, and it's always right around the old man's anniversary. He brings a few of his buddies over to this bar a mile off the interstate (called The Elephant Room on account of this trophy bull (with tusks have to be eight feet long) they got hung up near the ceiling, and supposedly the owner's grandad bought it from some kid way back when (or maybe he shot it himself (with a rifle he stole from Ernest Hemingway)), though for all we know it could be synthetic, could have been made by some eight-year-old on the outskirts of Shanghai, and maybe they keep bringing in new ones at regular intervals just so it all looks fresh and impressive and manly), and they drink a shot of Bushmills for every year of marriage (this last time it was 32 (which meant they each had eight (and felt frothy and bleary and alive))), and he tells them all about how he didn't ask for no bachelor party, and that whole week before the wedding, he was mostly just wanting to be left alone, and his best man (whose name was Wilkes, but six years back, he drove all the way out to Council Bluffs just so he could take a header off the Bob Kerrey Pedestrian Bridge) sprang for a cheap motel room in Clear Lake, right across the street from the Surf Ballroom. Then Wilkes gave him a couple of sixers and a stack of dirty magazines and told him to lock the door and think about Buddy Holly and winter dance parties and all that life-is-fragile bullshit, and now's the time for reflection and probably your last shot to bail, and here the old man likes to add some color, to fill in some details about how the walls were paper thin, and these two assholes next door were breaking bottles and fighting about Wall Street and Ronald Reagan, and what the old man did was stay up all night drinking and looking at pictures of naked women (this was 1988, so the women all had these perms fanned out six inches from their heads and natural tits and names like way-out Western cities, names like Odessa and Cheyenne and Phoenix) and think to himself, "Shit, I got the Trans Am parked outside, and it's got a full tank and working AC, and 80 goes all the way to California and 35 to Texas, and if the women look like this, then what am I doing in Iowa, and who the fuck would miss me, anyway," and for hours he packed and then re-packed (and once even got as far as the driver's seat) and nearly did go AWOL, nearly let it all go, and some years (depending on the weather or the politics or the price of corn) he tells his buddies that he probably should have, and other times he calls the act of sticking around his biggest regret (and one night (which must have been year 26 or 27) he told the whole bar he figured Wilkes had it right, and maybe he should head for the ol' Bob Kerrey himself), and when he's done, they all raise a glass (and the friends always turn sober and sanguine and serious, and they look directly at that old bull with politeness, with hollow Mid-western courtesy (and also that weighty dread that comes with ritual)), and they tell him it ain't too late, that there's still time, and, listen, buddy, you could up and leave tomor-row, and the fact of the matter is you never amounted to much, is no one's really gonna miss you now.

True Crime

S omebody killed an undercover in that half-collapsed barn off 29, and for a while me and Cliff were telling people we went out there the very next night. Two in the morning. Three. Once we said five, and we talked about dawn coming on and feeling seasick and excited, and Cliff parked the car just outside the tape, and we fucked in the back seat. Sometimes we said screwed. Or got busy. Fooled around like back in high school, and it depended on how we were feeling. Who was the audience and how many beers deep. We said we heard crickets, and I had my face pressed against the window (or the tape deck or the dash), and George Strait was on the radio, or Buddy Holly, and when it was over, we threw the condom into the field along with some shell casings or heroin (or oftentimes both), and we watched it all land near some torn-up shingles, then gunned it like mad. We drove like hell. We laughed and danced and didn't sleep for another 12 hours, and sometimes it was more like 19, and then we got real high, and maybe we said we went out there the next night and did it all over again.

People would be looking at us by then. Blinking and laughing real nervous while we downed the rest of our beers. Somebody would always ask what happened next, and we'd say, nothing much, but maybe the story wasn't over. Maybe we were still waiting. Then, there'd be this wild Iowa silence, and someone would get up the nerve to ask what we were waiting for, and Cliff would look him right in the eye and tell him we were waiting for the cops. Waiting for cameras. We were role-playing interviews and hearings and headlines, and what we were waiting for was confrontation, our guaranteed day in televised, all-American court.

Dead Celebrity Bingo

We'd throw these parties, and everyone would dress like dead celebrities, and we'd pass out bingo cards with Buddy Holly as the free space. Sometimes Ritchie Valens. We tried the Big Bopper once, but nobody knew who the fuck he was, and the whole thing landed just exactly like that plane they put him on, and we sure learned our lesson good. Sometimes some asshole English major would show up with a paper bag over his head and say he was Thomas Pynchon, but whatever kind of joke that was I never really understood, and the worst was that time the feminists came. Carrie Chapman Catt and Margaret Sanger and somebody they said was named Daniella Flores-Whitaker, and they all sat in a circle in the basement. They weren't even in a sorority. Nobody invited them, and all they did was stare and hold hands and read passages from, I don't know, this book that sounded boring as shit, and we could not get drunk enough to drown it out. They left around midnight. And then Bill fell down the stairs and landed on a broken bottle. Had to get his face stitched up, and the nurse asked us if Tom Petty was really dead or if it was all some kind of sick prank, and then they kicked three brothers out of school that semester, and nobody would tell us the reason why. I think I met Alma right around then, too, and she's out in Utah now and shacked up with that limp-dick cowboy who rides bulls on ESPN2 at 3 in the morning, and we all still meet up over at Buddy's in Mason City and talk about it every once in a while. It gets late. We smoke outside. Somebody mentions King Tut and dead canaries and poison mosquitos, and there's a full moon. We stare at it until it looks like a baseball, and nobody says nothing out loud, but we're all thinking it, and what it is is things was a lot better before that night, weren't they, and them women must've been into voodoo. I bet they put some kind of hex on us all.

Cerro Gordo County Tourism Bureau

There was this documentary (that aired exclusively on-line (and even then some outlets took it down, and it got to the point where you had to look real hard, really had to know what you're doing)) that claimed Buddy Holly was not actually dead, and neither was Ritchie Valens (and not the Big Bopper, either), or, well, it could have been that they were dead, but it didn't happen on no airplane, and it sure as shit wasn't 1959, and that whole Surf Ballroom mythology was invented by some hotshot in tourism. Somebody by the name of Fillmore, it said. Got a buddy to get a mannequin all dinged up (and slipped some old busted horn-rims into a snowbank 100 feet away) and then wrecked this Beechcraft Bonanza he got from some collector (or sometimes Howard Hughes) and just invited the newspaper out to take pictures (and, of course, they did it all gleeful and believing because that was the story of a lifetime right there (and the cops and the coroner weren't about to be the bad guys, and maybe they sensed opportunity, too)), and Buddy Holly and Valens and the ol' Bopper, well, they knew enough just to shut right up and disappear because death makes people famous, don't it? And it's like van Gogh, maybe. Or that Kafka, and if you look real close, the whole thing makes a lot of sense. Because the story got big after a while. They wrote songs about it. Musicals. Movies. And people poured into the middle of nowhere Iowa and sang dirges in the dark and all that jazz, and the only thing about this documentary that was remotely crazy (and even it seems only natural if you really want to consider it) was this idea that came in at the end, and it was that the story about the whole crash being fake (as in, the entire argument indulged in by this particular documentary) was itself (knowingly and intentionally) invented (sometime in those early 2000s, or maybe 2010s) by some guy named Warren Hafner while he was on a jag with the hotel company trying to buy out the land and get zoning licenses and build that fancy resort they got up on the alleged "crash" site, and he did it because the only thing more lucrative than a death shrine is a goddamn conspiracy (and a real death/fake death/was-it-a-setup conspiracy especially (and just look at what they did with Kennedy)), and I heard an interview on the radio. IPR, I think. The host sounded like her nose was pinched (or jammed straight into the air), and she asked this guy from the Cerro Gordo County Tourism Bureau, she goes, "Well, was there really a plane crash, and, if there was, then what do you make of this sort of accusation that private interests [and it's, like, here implied just somehow in her tone that the county authorities (and could be it's the whole State of Iowa) are maybe complicit, too] are engaged in a kind of anti-reality, alternative history propaganda campaign to bring in some extra travel dollars, and, well, what I mean is, how do we sort the truth here?" (which is all convoluted as hell, but then what do you expect from regional radio?), and the guy from tourism (you can tell), he just sits there for a while. Absorbs some dead air. His chair creaks, and he gets real focused. Real wild-eyed, and what he says is something like: "I wasn't around back then, and I can't say for sure, either way, but I never heard anyone actually from here say the whole Buddy Holly story was anything other than gospel truth, and they made movies about it, didn't they, and as for who started which rumor and who funded this documentary you're talking about, it all seems pretty simple to me. Because these listeners, they got eyes. And they got cars. And if anyone wants to 'sort the truth,' like you said, well, tell 'em to come on down to Cerro Gordo County. It's real pretty in the summer, real corn-fed and American, and there's some stories manage to make it big, and this one here's real layered and all tied up with them ghosts of rock 'n' roll, and, look. This is the point. There's some things I can't help you with. Some stories you gotta see for yourself."

Exposure Therapy

My cousin Gregory was scared to death of crickets. Petrified. Could barely go outside in the summer, and, at night, he had to sleep with the TV on and three fans going, and if one little chirp managed to leak through the window, he'd pull the covers up over his head and practically shit himself. That was why Uncle Lenny drank so goddamn much, everyone said, and the whole situation was a mess, and one night we drove Gregory out to Mystic Lanes in Mason City. Told him we were going bowling. Except we had these three old canning jars in the trunk, and they were full of crickets, and Lipmann brought 'em all inside in his league bag, and, right around the seventh frame, we just let the freaks run free. Middle of Gregory's turn. They're chirping and fiddling and what have you, and some youth-group girls are screaming and praying, and I swear to Christ they all started chanting the Our Father, and Gregory, he fucking nearly passed out. Just straight crumpled. Sat there only halfway breathing, and as he's lying there twitching, the bugs are crawling all up and down his arms and legs. One of 'em is, like, pawing at his teeth. Lipmann, he's cracking jokes about Chinese fucking delicacies, and Old Man Hicks is at the counter about to call 911, when "Maybe Baby" comes on over the speakers, and the whole thing gets pretty fucking surreal. Like one of them slow-motion movies. Gregory looks pale as shit. Lipmann is telling him to get his ass up, and the whole time I'm figuring, well, this is pretty much it, isn't it, and either he dies right there in the gutter, or he ends up owing us just about the world's biggest favor, and I don't know where he is now, but sometimes somebody gets a postcard marked Idaho or fucking Utah, and alls I can see is Gregory on his back. He's looking up at Mormon sky. Trying not to drown in that Great Salt Lake.

Nuclear Medicine Man

Warren Hafner gives a couple interviews a year to these hospitality trade pubs (there was one in *Lodging* a few months back if you need, like, some kind of a for-instance), and he always talks about this B&B he used to run back when he was a kid. Fresh from college. Got an angel (with deep pockets and even deeper connections to both the federal government and the Benton County zoning authorities) and bought this fleet of Winnebago Chieftains and parked them 30 feet apart along Route 240 in Washington (overlooking the old Hanford Site) and put up these big signs all over the Seattle, Spokane, Portland, and Boise metros, and there were photos of mushroom clouds. Missile silos. One of them (he always says it was along I-84 or I-5 or out by the Yakama Reservation, and he can never remember where exactly (or, at least, that's what he claims)) featured a *Brady Bunch*-style collage, only instead of Jan and Peter and the gang, there were images of birth defects and tumors the size of your head, and there was this one picture of a dog with, like, six legs and half a face (and, believe it or not (he says), that was the one people found most disturbing (based on focus-group data he collected himself)), and there's always mention in some kind of parenthetical aside about how he (meaning Hafner) still believes some of these billboards were responsible for, like, multicar pileups and fender benders, and he somehow manages both to point out that there were "certainly no deaths" and to joke about adding thousands of dollars (in post-wreck premiums) to the tills of auto insurance companies all around the Pacific Northwest (not to mention to the economy writ large). He called the place the Isotope Inn, and it was this oddball destination for freaks and weirdos and the kind of tourist with a taste for coming face-to-face with death (this is what Hafner made a career on, and if he's got a personal mission statement, it's most definitely something like: "Your average vacationer wants his ass kissed, but the richest ones, well, they want theirs good and kicked"), and the idea was basically just to sit around with some special choice beverage and look out at the most radioactive spot in the United States. To take in the stars and breathe real deep and imagine the levels of atomic decay straight pumping through the air and the dirt, and this was all perfectly safe, mind you, but he supplied bottles of water (including some marked with the skull and crossbones as, like, an experiment) and lead jackets and made his guests sign this waiver a foot-and-a-half thick (though he claims most of it was blank) and generally just invited them to picture. To sit there feeling the cancer creep into their skins. Of course, there's no real evidence the place actually existed (except for a few old internet pages (archived by the Wayback Machine) listing a defunct phone number and several photos that appear to have been doctored), but hospitality message boards are filled with folks who claim they stayed there once or twice back in their vagabond days (and replies that accuse them of having been hired by Hafner himself (and the whole thing generally dissolves into flame wars and all-caps rant-a-thons)), and some of them say they really did turn up with cancer (then there are whole threads featuring nothing but lengthy meditations on causality and coincidence, on the assumption of risk and the fundamental principles of informed consent), and the point is, well, it's all become part of the Hafner mystique, and he says he disbanded the thing after one summer because he got his money back plus a tidy sum, and, anyway, that kind of shit is better abbreviated. Better scarce. Better disappearing into legend, and he ends every interview by talking about that last night he slept out there and how it was a full moon, and he took this little stroll into the restricted area (sometimes it's just to the very edge; sometimes it's all the way out to the old Hanford High) and saw more sky than he'd ever seen in his life, and he swears to Christ the crickets were the size of iguanas. Like, the moths were fucking glowing, and they kept zooming around his ears and making this sound like nothing he's ever heard (he describes it as these sort of vaguely Xhosa clicks mixed with, like, a lawn mower in desperate need of an oil change), and the whole time he's drinking Tanqueray and tasting pine needles and thinking, like, what could be more American than this, and he always tells the interviewer the only thing he can think of is sleeping in some oak-floored room with custom furniture and marble countertops, and you're surrounded by pictures of Chief Joseph and Geronimo and Tecumseh (or maybe the Shawnee Prophet), and the whole thing's part of this luxury condo complex built on top of an old Indian burial ground (or maybe (and he only said this once, and it was in *Beaten Path* (which almost no one reads)) just right directly over Wounded Knee (or Sand Creek (or near Bear River (or all along the Trail of Tears)))) and paying two grand for just the one night's pleasure, and maybe there's peyote included or some kind of mystical sweat-lodge guided tour, and what an idea, he says, and I've always wanted to do it, and (even in print) you can tell he's looking right directly through this reporter who's asking him questions (and into the eyes of the reading public) and saying, like, that's the kind of destination we're about to set up, so get out your credit card. Because it'll be here sooner than you can possibly think.

Road to Damascus

Nobody knows what exactly happened to the Fenwick kid, but he's gone and got real religious. Started hanging around at Mystic Lanes over in Mason City. Getting friendly with the youth groups on cosmic nights. Ordering and then nursing these Shirley Temples, and every so often he'll find one of them little women wants to try and save the world (or at least some man (or, in Fenwick's case, boy, more like) can't figure out how to live in it), and she'll roll on over to his lane, and they'll talk about the Beatitudes or the Good Samaritan, and maybe she'll say she loves the Gospel of John, and he'll tell her he's more of a Luke man, and there's that moment where Jesus goes out to the desert. Doesn't eat nothing for 40 days. The Devil's with him. Says, listen, man, J. C., I got a real sweet deal for you, and this Fenwick kid probably tells her he's been there. Metaphorically, he means. Maybe physically. And one night he was at this party in Clear Lake just all kinds of screwed up on intoxicants, and everyone was dressed like dead celebrities, and he's pretty sure he was John Wayne, and somehow, by the grace of God (because he knows there's no such thing as coincidence (least not if you're a true believer)), he meets these two shamans carrying holy water in a couple of mason jars, and the stuff burns like hell going down, but that's the point, I guess, he says. It's got to hurt to purify, and, anyway, these guys (or the truth of it is they could've been angels, he says, and they walk among us, and the reality is you'd never really know), they take him over to this place way out in the middle of nowhere, and it's this cornfield that smells like gasoline, and he swears it's like one of them vision quests, and he sees all kinds of things. The girl's nodding along by now. They've stopped bowling. Middle of the seventh frame. The kids from the youth group two lanes over aren't staring full-on (they're too polite for that), but some of them have managed to perfect the side-eye. Watching out for their friend because Fenwick, he looks a little off his meds these days (even if he wasn't ever on any to begin with (not that we know of, anyway (though, of course, you know how it is with that whole generation and the Adderall and the Ritalin, not to mention the anxiety disorders and trigger warnings and all-around mental fucking fragility))), and the youth-group kids probably think he's gonna try to take her out back and get her to smoke up or shoot up or something worse, like he's gonna try to get her to commit some kind of cardinal, mortal, deadly sin (and you can bet some of them sort of secretly hope he does, just for the drama of it), but all he's really doing is saying how he passed out in that field and saw these lights. Thought he was gonna get abducted by aliens or raptured right then and there, but what it was was St. Blaise, and he's wearing these horn-rimmed glasses and some pinstripe suit, and you remember him, right? He's the guy with the throats. Tells Fenwick he's got to use his. To preach and spread the word and tell everyone he can find not to up and leave this town because it's still something special here, something magic, and the whole of Cerro Gordo County's the kind of place that's Blessed and Sacred and marked by Jesus Himself for Glory and Resurrection when we get to them End Times, and the Lord Jehovah (or maybe it's Elohim (or just pure and simple God)), He's been sending signs and wonders ever since that plane fell from the sky in 1959, and that's why Fenwick quit college. Lives in his mom's basement. Sometimes he passes out fliers on the corner by the Dairy Queen or puts them on cars parked over at the Fareway, and someday soon he's gonna start his own website. Email newsletter. Might even buy some wood and build a one-room church on this property some cousin of his owns up near Freeman, and hold nightly meetings, and maybe she'll want to come and preach. That, or they could become missionaries together and ride the open road and go farmhouse-to-farmhouse and sleep in some RV they buy used from his stepdad or maybe one of her uncles, and about then, she edges away because she finally fucking sees it. We all see it. And everybody's got these little wagers on where young Fenwick's really gonna end up, and most of us say all methed out somewhere off Highway 18, or maybe OD'd on Percs in the alley back behind the Walgreens, and there's others think they'll find him hitchhiking in Utah 20 years from now, looking for patterns in them little prairie dog clicks or hoping to join the Mormons and get in on some of that polygamy action, and there's some optimistic (or, well, I call 'em naïve) folks think he can get over it. Like, as in, the whole thing will pass like some phase, and he'll end up finishing school or at least an associate's over at the community college, and could be he'll work at a bank. Lumber yard. Maybe he'll get a job with some ag company in Ankeny or suburban Omaha (or up near them Twin Cities if he's real lucky), and then he'll be just like everybody else, and that gets the entire county thinking because that's pretty much the whole wide range of options, anyway. With or without the cornfield messiah and real dramatic visions, and it kind of makes you wonder, don't it? If his whole bullshit story counts as any kind of conversion at all.

Caucus Night

That was the last time Fillmore got really drunk, and we didn't even vote. Just wandered around some miniature gymnasium collecting buttons and stickers and all kinds of other shit, and Fillmore told one of them precinct captains she was a dead ringer for that one governor or mayor or what was it. The sexy one. From Alaska. Looked her dead in the eye and said, you might be prettier, even. Like you could maybe be Miss North Dakota, at the very least.

She didn't say nothing. Gave him a look like, get the fuck out, basically, and that's pretty much exactly what we did. Everyone was standing around fiddling with cards, anyway, and we went out to the parking lot and drank even more. Might have been gin. Jim Beam. Or that beer we got on discount, 30 of 'em for 18 bucks, and there were these real big American flags plastered all over the whole fucking can. Fillmore ripped off his shirt. Stood on the roof of this old Cutlass he got from some guy down the block. He stuck them stickers all up and down his chest, and he looked like Rambo without any ammunition, or like some kind of bad-ass Boy Scout, on account of it was 25 degrees and he's not shivering at all, and then people started filing on out. Most of them didn't even bother to look. Fillmore kept yelling about how he was the picture of democracy, and, if anyone wanted to take a real selfie with a real American, well, then they could step right on up. Of course, no one did. Except this group of high schoolers, and they must've been observing, or else these kids just look younger and softer all the time, and they stopped about 20 feet short. Took out their phones. They kept pointing and clicking for 30 seconds had to be, maybe a full minute, and the whole time they're laughing and sort of half-screaming, and with every touch these flashes went off, and it looked like fireworks. Explosions. Like Buddy Holly's plane heading for nowhere, and that happened in February, too, and for, like, a split second the world felt huge and wide and open, and here's our empty old Iowa just right smack in the middle of the scene.

Kayfabe

Three years after the divorce came through, I asked Gloria if she ever thought about getting back on the old horse, and she said she only had room in her life for two men. One of them was me. The other was this guy she went to high school with, this guy whose parents named him Buddy Hooley, and maybe it was destiny, or it could have been desperation, but he ended up a small-town professional wrestler. Did these underground shows in Dubuque and Waterloo and Marshalltown where he'd take dumbbells to the skull. Get tossed on thumbtacks. He used his real name and entered the ring to Weezer after some promoter said "Oh Boy!" didn't have enough bass, and Hooley carried this cheap imitation Les Paul that always wound up smashed, and sometimes it was over his own head after the referee had been knocked out or otherwise kicked aside. Gloria said Hooley's signature move was called the "Big Bopper," and it involved climbing to the top rope and doing this kind of whirling splash attack with his body all perpendicular, and one night she watched him at this show in Mason City, or could've been Clear Lake, and, anyway, it was right along I-35, and they had Hooley in the main event against some guy who wore sagging pants and called himself Prince Cheese. It was a back-and-forth match, she said. Both guys used the razor blades. There's blood on the canvas, popcorn, broken glass from a beer bottle Cheese stole from some asshole in the front row, and sometime toward the end, Hooley climbs up to the top rope. Someone tosses him the guitar. Cheese is staggering around in the middle of the ring, and, come to think of it, Hooley's woozy and off-balance, too, only he's perched in the more precarious spot, and he kind of half-launches himself and half-slips, and next thing you know, he's falling in the wrong direction. Going headlong toward the concrete. Gloria sees him land dome first, and she says there's this sound like a ring toss, like a woodpecker, and he does not move for five, 10 seconds, and the last thing anyone sees is two of the other performers, these guys some people say were dressed like Ritchie Valens or Elvis Presley, and they drag Hooley out the back entrance while the referee raises Cheese's hand and declares Cheese the winner, and the crowd is stunned silence. Is nobody knows what the fuck. And they don't see Hooley afterward, either. Not for weeks. Not for forever, and he doesn't do any more shows, and he never answers his phone, but Gloria says his voicemail still works, and she swears the message changes just slightly, and it's not the words exactly but the sound, the cadence, the way it feels like he's talking to her, and as far as she can tell, there's no death certificate, no county autopsy, and some people think the promoter buried the body out near the actual crash site, and some say it was all planned, all scripted and theatrics, and Gloria, she doesn't know what to believe. She knows her phone rings sometimes. Number unknown. There's nothing but static when she picks up. Heavy breathing. Rock 'n' roll all soft and haunted in the background, and she wonders if it's him on the other end, or maybe the promoter. She wonders what's real. She looks at me, and it's like the first night we met, and her eyes are green, and they look 10 years younger, and she says, "Tex, I can't wake up." And, "Everything feels like it's part of the show."

Photo Ops

Some politicians visit all 99 counties, and some just hit the hot spots. Maid-Rite and Dubuque Street and the Iowa State Fair. Then there are the years where some fad pops up, small-town coffee shops or welding plants or that time everyone paid a visit to those monks who make the caskets, and once, I remember, it was the Buddy Holly crash site. This was because of some big anniversary, and maybe it was 45 or maybe it was 65, and, either way, it was before they built that hotel out there, and there were a truckload of candidates that cycle. Both parties. Thirty or possibly 40, and every last one of 'em took a picture, and they got them all framed in this collage on the wall over at Buddy's in Mason City, and it looks like presidential Hollywood Squares, and the old-timers like to sit and drink Brandy Old-Fashioneds like they grew up in Wisconsin. They stare at them photos and crack jokes because all the politicians, they somehow got different looks. The women, generally, are more likely to smile, even if it ain't toothy. They got their arms around somebody. They look like they are trying to learn. Then there are the old guys, and they got clenched jaws and straight-ahead stares, and you get this feeling like they're leading the camera into battle, like they think they're MacArthur or Patton or maybe just George C. Scott, and sometimes, the drunker they get, the old-timers recreate all them campaign conversations. One guy plays the chair. Somebody else is some secondary aide, and then there's this chorus of spokesperson surrogate voices, and what it sounds like is, "Well, say, do you think he should smile a little, Joe?"

Then, "Nah. Too much history. Too many ghosts."

"Better off trying to look presidential."

"Prize-fighterly."

"A smile is a fucking insult, I tell ya, and we want him lookin' like Joe Louis or Ali or Rocky Marciano, and exactly who probably depends on, like, age and ethnicity, don't it?"

"Yeah, or, like, personal preference, and, if it were me, I'd want to be Jake LaMotta, but more like Robert De Niro, if you know what I mean."

"Or, if the candidate's young, like that what's-his-name there, then maybe it's like, listen, son, we want you looking like Kennedy. Like Bobby. Or Old Ted just after that Chappaquiddick."

"Like you're just a hound dog. You ain't never done nothing wrong in your life."

"Be like Reagan. But cowboy Reagan. 'Win one for the Gipper' Reagan. Knute Rockne, All-American."

"Nah, what it really is is we want you touching some old farmer. Some guy and his wife straight out of that painting, and nothing creepy or nothing, but just, like, a steady hand on the arm, like you're guiding them, or better yet, like they're guiding you, and that'll really get the local yokels, won't it? Make 'em think they're the ones in charge, like they have total control," and everyone laughs at that, and it feels like a game, but the truth is a lot of people voted based on those photos that year. They talked about it down at the precincts on caucus night, and there were buttons and pennants all over the goddamn place, and, during the realignment, I'm telling you, people pulled these pictures out of their fucking wallets. They went around and asked if you were really going for that sourpuss, or them red cheeks, or that one-eyebrowed woman with the gaping mouth, or that wet-behind-the-ears preener with the shit-eating grin and no goddamn respect, and that's really who you want to throw your weight behind? All that power, and you're gonna spend it on him? On her? On some idiot probably thinks Buddy Holly played with a trio of actual mutant crickets or something, and what a goddamn waste. Except, of course, the young folks always thought the real waste was reducing an entire platform to one frameable moment, and they filled up all them gyms with talk of airbrushing and social-media sanitization and something called "doing it for the 'Gram," and some of us, and maybe here I mean yours truly, we actually thought they were talking about cocaine, if you can believe it, but the point is there's some of them still around. Not many, but a few. These folks is real cynical, and they think it's all marketing, and one photo can't tell you nothing, but you ask most of us, you ask the guys over at Buddy's, we know better. Because this whole town's got the crash site burned into its memory. When we look out on that corn, even today, even though they got full parking lots and waterslides and license plates from all across this great country, all we see is wreckage. Debris. Some of us can still picture Buddy Holly himself laying there. We remember when they found his smashed-up glasses, and if you really want our opinion, what we'll tell you is this. Laugh all you want. But you look in the eyes of them photos, and you remember. Whatever you see, that's who's in the cockpit. That's what's flying this whole goddamn plane.

The Searchers

I spent the summer visiting dead places. Effigy Mounds and the Buddy Holly crash site and some nothing Nebraska nowhere with cars stacked up like Stonehenge. It looked reasonably exact. In Utah, I met a Mormon on the side of the road, and he had green eyes and wore a full suit, and we drove to St. George while he talked forever about radiation. Thyroid cancer. Wind patterns and exposure lawsuits and labyrinthine acts of Congress, and he said John Wayne died out here. "Not exactly," he said. "But cells are a time bomb, and this is the place that started his clock."

"It's beautiful," I said.

"You just have to know how to look." There were canyons and megachurches, and everything seemed red. Red rocks. Red sky. Red clouds. For a minute I thought it was Mars. I dropped him on the steps of the courthouse, and "Go on, now," he said. "Ride them highways and preach," and I had no idea what he meant, but that's exactly what I did. I bought 12 copies of the Book of Mormon and figured I'd cruise 15 and hit the Strip. Live Hollywood. The Pacific. Or I'd drive out to the Nevada Test Site and take one of the tours, and maybe I'd sneak off. Find some quiet spot and bury myself in the dirt and then just nibble on it, put it in my pockets and lug it around and let it breathe through my skin, and this is how you become a man, I thought. This is a Western. It's as close as you'll ever get to John Marion Morrison Wayne.

The Quiet Man

McQuaid was my best man, and he rode shotgun while I cashed that first alimony check. Friday morning. We took PTO and flirted with the bank teller. Asked her if she wanted to take a ride out to the John Wayne birthplace and then maybe get our britches tangled, and you could tell she was pissed but acting real polite like how most women do, and that was all fine with us because she looked like a drip, anyhow. A real fucking wet blanket, and all we needed was the cooler full of Yoo-hoo and Busch and the bags full of Old Dutch potato chips, and we found a Lion's Den off 35 and cruised box covers, and there was this one that looked exactly like Lana, only darker. More curves. Better shape. The model's name was Laramie, and we'd both seen her stuff before, and she was wearing this Old West outfit with the shirt about to break wide open like a Texas prairie. Like golden Kansas wheat. We bought her and then pulled out the insert and taped it to the back window like some kind of war flag, and we'd race past truckers, and they'd lay on the horn, and I think we figured maybe we'd watch the movie when we got on back home, but I don't know that we ever did, and mostly we called each other Pilgrim and took pictures underneath the statue. Stood up there all casual like the Duke and dodged dirty looks. Gave him a drink. We drove around Winterset and found one of them old covered bridges of Madison County and threw beer cans into some half-empty riverbed, then listened while they splashed and rattled and rolled.

"To them high-strung feminists," McQuaid said, and we toasted their asses. Tits, too. He said if this is what all that women's lib was about, then we should've got ourselves on board years ago, and better late than never, I said. Let them rule the world and put us out to pasture, and "I like this one right here," he said, and we stayed out until the moon got big. It hit our faces. Something howled, and it could have been a coyote or maybe it was a wolf, and this was the revolution, we thought. This was the brave new world, and I still can't remember how it ended. How we ever even managed to get ourselves on back to the car.

Uncanny Valley

The whole of Cerro Gordo County's internet traffic gets routed through (and then stored on) some NSA server in suburban fucking Utah (of all places), and 19.59 percent of it is porn (with most of that coming from about two dozen guys (all of whom have tastes that run fairly vanilla, and, for some reason, an eight-year-old video clip featuring (a (then) 22-year-old) Laramie Voyeur in an FFM scene involving (for some reason) cowboy hats and poodle skirts gets accessed at least twice a week, and it's always different IPs, and (from the looks of it) none of them have even communicated with one another, and this has the analysis algos (not to mention the techs (when they even bother to look)) thoroughly confused)), and a (surprisingly) even higher portion is tourists stuck in some cornfield 12 miles off the interstate and trying to use their phones to get directions to the Buddy Holly crash site, and, of course, there's dating sites. Baseball scores. Longform essays (and some (very) short stories) that get accessed but (the analysis algos can tell) never read (at least not deeply (based on time spent and scrolling patterns and screenshots featuring dozens of simultaneously opened tabs)). Point being is this. Is that most of it's harmless. Junk. Utterly useless from a surveillance perspective (though perhaps not an entertainment one (at least on the (very) rare occasions when an actual human happens to be watching)), except that some of it gets simultaneously scraped by various data brokerage or psychoanalytic firms, and sometimes good old Uncle Sam catches somebody looking up instructions for explosives. How much fertilizer, etc. Maybe they find some idiot in a dive motel room right across from the Surf, and he's researching Timothy McVeigh and purchasing copy upon copy of *The Turner Diaries* and (from all appearances) contemplating some kind of agro-terrorist arson while also accessing all sorts of radical leftist manifestos, including that one by Ted Kaczynski (and it could be that one or the other of these search records is fabricated, a doubling back, an attempt to throw the whole intelligence community off the scent (though (approximately) nobody thinks this Midwestern halfwit's got the mental aptitude to manage that)), and the upshot is that his whole web history looks like the ramblings of a madman. A writer, maybe. Researching some deeply unreadable (and probably never-to-be-written) book, and the true level of threat is easy enough to figure. A trigger gets tripped, and then a software program (code name: HAWKEYE PIERCE) does basically everything else. It's seamlessly embedded into this motel asshole's machine (which is a Dell Inspiron 14 5000) and then eventually shared with all his other devices (or, well, just one device, really, and it's this ancient, fourth-generation iPhone that doesn't even have the latest software updates), and this program collects everything and searches for patterns and even features an (experimental) retinal scanner that uses pupil illumination and darting speed and infrared imaging (designed to detect corneal blood-flow patterns) to measure the guy's emotional responses (his levels of hostility and interest and arousal) as he's browsing, and then it uses a fairly rudimentary profiling algo to make the following recommendation: Subject, though legitimately angry (for no concretely discernible reason (though his information-consumption patterns closely align with those of members of various Western libertarian organizations, most especially a Wyoming group (previously known to the Agency) called Liberty Valance, whose entire mission appears to be the opening up of federally owned grasslands for private grazing and ranching, and they've staged a number of (heretofore entirely peaceful) sit-ons in and around Yellowstone National Park)), lacks the psycho-emotional makeup necessary for engagement with deviant criminal behavior and is most likely committed to participation in an elaborate game of chicken, whereby his entire digital existence is employed to capture the attention of domestic intelligence authorities in the hopes of provoking a confrontation (which he sees as potentially cathartic, as (finally) allowing for the opportunity to address his (though he imagines they're widely shared) grievances to a power structure that he sees as both intentionally faceless and unreachable) without the mess of collateral casualties, and, while he will continue to search for "red flag" information (and may even purchase the various supplies necessary for the creation of violent instruments (most likely amateurish Molotov cocktails and souped-up fireworks and imitation dynamite utilizing an ammonium-nitrate base)), there is a 97 percent chance it will never escalate beyond mere flirtation, and, even in the unlikely event that life circumstances (e.g. exposure to highly immersive, graphically violent (and intensely social) media, terminal illness, etc.) alter his personality in such a way as to make him more amenable to criminal activity, there's an 89 percent chance (given the life expectancy figures for a white, overweight (borderline obese), male smoker (genetically predisposed to both heart disease and various forms of colorectal cancer (including several known to be particularly aggressive) from rural Iowa (and living (at least temporarily) in a building that features asbestos insulation, lead paint and pipes, and levels of radon requiring extensive mitigation))) he'll be dead before engaging in anything that would necessitate human intervention initiated by the Agency, let alone interrogation, let alone (preemptive or otherwise) arrest, and some dogs are old and sick, and the ratio of resource input to damage prevention renders any action in this particular case unnecessary, as well as fiscally undesirable.

Surf Ballroom Bliss

Friday after Thanksgiving, I meet this college girl over at Buddy's in Mason City. Has to be going on 2 a.m. She's on break. ISU, I think, or maybe it was UNI, and I don't remember too good, but she looks like Sandra Bullock if Sandra Bullock spent, like, her whole day walking through cow shit, and this is what Fillmore would call cornfield-sexy. Feedlot-sexy, and we're drinking Jack & 7s, and she says, "You know, I've always been an oldies kind of gal."

"Shit, sweetheart," I say. "I probably know your old man."

She scoffs. "A lot better than me, I bet. That asshole left when I was 10."

"Your old lady, then. Or some cousin or uncle or something, and I never been one to go asking for trouble. Finds me on its own sometimes, but this here's a whole other kettle of fish."

"I can keep a secret," she says, and, so, okay, I tell her, I'm drunk, and I always had this fantasy of sneaking into the Surf late at night and screwing on the dance floor and pretending the wood's like sand on a beach. Feeling the varnish on my ass. Imagining all three of them rockers up there watching from the stage, and I'm looking at this torn-up, moldy carpet by about halfway through, but she says she's up for it. Says it sounds like a blast. Only thing is we better get a bottle to go, she tells me, and they do off-sale here, right, and you bet, I say, and so we grab some Jack for the road, and she takes pulls the whole way down 18. I get a couple of swigs at stoplights. Put the Cutlass in park and rev the engine. The Surf's locked up pretty good when we get there, but she says, "There's always a back door" all suggestive, and what it ends up being this time is a window. I rip my jeans on the ledge.

Inside, the place is dead dark. You can't hear nothing. Footsteps echo like bats up in the attic, and we start in this booth that's sponsored by some dive motel off 35, but then it gets cramped, and we move down to the dance floor for a while. Our eyes adjust, and maybe we can see each other, or maybe it's just shadows, and she tells me she's gonna move up to Milwaukee after graduation, and that's probably the best she can do.

"Milwaukee's nice," I say.

"I can waitress."

"Work at the ballpark."

"Just midnight shift somewhere, and I like how the neon looks when it gets real late at night."

"I'll come visit on weekends. Maybe we'll cruise the lake."

"We can do that here," she says, and she's right.

I tell her, I say, "Hon, all these places, you know they're just exactly the same."

I want her to lean in right then because I ain't making the first move, not in no situation like this, but all she does is tap her foot on the floor. She looks 17 all of a sudden, only all hardened up like those girls with the nose rings, and I think I have one of them out-of-body experiences. Like I can watch me watching her watch the stage, and maybe it's some long-gone rock 'n' roll ghost, or the liquor and adrenaline, and I reach for her hand. End up hitting nothing but wrist.

"Moment's passed, ain't it?" I say.

She looks at me straight on. Puts her nose right on mine. "Yeah," she says. "And you look like a guy who knows this already, but there's nothing we can do to bring any of it back."

The Bloody Holly Story

It starts on youth-group night at the Surf, and it's one of them up-till-dawn lock-ins with music and games and pretzels, and this is the mid-90s, but the girls are wearing poodle skirts. Ponytails. Guys have greased hair and white T-shirts with decks of cards rolled up under the sleeves, and the speakers are alternating between Tommy James and Elvis and this, like, soft-rock Christian music where the singers invoke Jesus by His actual name (all tender and sincere and earnest), and the kids dance far apart (except for the ones who sit close in the booths, looking deeply into each other's eyes and fidgeting with promise rings and saying how they'll be together forever, and just wait till we turn 18, and we can get married right then), and some of them sing with their eyes closed. There's this low-humming debate about whether you need to say grace before you reach in for a snack. No, is the consensus. But some of them do. And this girl (who they say is named Laura) goes to the bathroom on a dare, and she's supposed to say "Bloody Holly" 59 times while staring into the mirror, and nobody knows what happens (on account of it's just her in there), but when she comes out, she's holding this pair of horn-rimmed glasses with the lenses all busted, and they ain't polycarbonate. They sure seem like real glass. Some kids, they think they can see designs in the cracks. A picture of Jesus or the Virgin Mary, or hey, maybe that's a guitar or an airplane (or three guys on a coastal train), and, in the meantime, Laura's just standing there shaking and shocked, and she says Buddy Holly appeared to her. Says he touched her shoulder. It felt dead and frozen (or maybe it started to burn). He told her there's nothing worse than dying young, and he's in purgatory, having to relive the crash every single night, and it hurts just the same every time and all the way through. She starts crying. Some of her friends rub her back. The kids don't know if she's serious, and there's a few think she's a prophet, and some others think she's made the whole thing up, and then there's this contingent that believes it's all just the work of the Devil, and what they oughta do is burn those glasses just as soon as possible, before this goes any further. Before it gets out of hand, and they argue over this for a while. The music keeps playing. It gets late. Laura, she bows out or zones out, and it's one of them things where they're all talking about her like she isn't even there, and finally someone says, "Let's pray on it," and they do, and about halfway through the Our Father, two kids stand up on opposite sides of the dance floor and say, "We should throw them in the lake," and it's (exactly) simultaneous, so everyone takes this as a sign. The chaperones (who are half- (or maybe fully) asleep at this point) let the kids out. They walk through the neighborhood. Maybe 50, 60 kids. It's all hushed whispers and footsteps, and, word is, if you overheard it, it would've sounded pretty damn mystical, and they make their way over to the pier. There's a whole line of kids. Standing. Staring at the Lady of the Lake, and Laura, they send her out to the edge of the dock, and she tosses the glasses in like a Frisbee, and (possibly another little miracle) everyone swears they hear the glasses sink. They all just stand there for a bit. Dead quiet. Nobody knows what to do, but it's this collective reverie, and the whole walk back to the Surf is silent. It's dawn by the time they get there, and parents are lined up in minivans and beat-up SUVs, and the kids, they all look shot. Exhausted. Basically beat to shit, and, of course, that figures (because they were up all night and drinking Jolt or Surge or Mountain Dew by the barrel), so no one asks any questions, and everyone goes home to sleep, but they still talk about it the next day and all through the weekend. All through the whole next year. Laura, she becomes, like, small-town famous, and it gets bad enough that (they say) she lights out the day after graduation and winds up living somewhere way up in the Nebraska Panhandle (or maybe it's Idaho (or sometimes Utah)), and warm days you can still see kids with snorkels at City Beach. Full diving gear. They'll tell you they're looking for Bloody Holly's glasses. In the distance, they can see older folks in boats, dumping in these old horn-rims from the Dollar General, and so there must be dozens of pairs under the water there (and when a kid finds one, the general rule is not to say shit, to hold the glasses close and hide them under the bed, and the whole idea is they'll bring good luck), and the boaters and the divers, they actually wave to each other. Smile. Raise a toast. They salute and pass this kind of mutual respect because the sun is shining, and the lake smells like fish and algae, and this is Clear Lake, and the whole thing is like baseball. Ritual. Legacy. Tradition. It's Cerro Gordo County's favorite summer pastime.

Beechcraft Bonanza

They had a story in the paper last week about a guy up in Kossuth County who built a Beechcraft Bonanza in his barn. A model, I mean. Full-size. Same one killed Buddy Holly, and it looked just perfect. Like it could actually fly. You wanted to climb inside when you saw the pictures. They said he got all the wood himself from these twisted old maples on down the property line, and he sanded it up real nice, then painted it red and white. Wrote "Winter Dance Party" all over port, or maybe it was starboard, or maybe pilots just use left and right, and how in the hell should I know, but the point is people came from all over. Not just the Midwest, either. There were cars parked out near this big empty soy field and all along P30, and the reporter, she went and scoped license plates. A lot were from Texas. One from Maine. She interviewed a family said they drove from Salt Lake City and did the whole trip just right straight through. Seventeen hours total on account of they pushed it to 90 all the way across Nebraska and stopped only for gas and so the kids could use the bathroom and buy M&M's and cheap sandwiches, and the wife said this was the greatest thing she'd ever seen. It was almost mystical, really, and was only one carpenter she could think of capable of that kind of work, and you know they hung Him up on a piece of wood Himself. Her husband apparently laughed when she said that. But otherwise, he was too busy staring and snapping photos to notice much else, and the kids were running through the fields, chasing a baseball, according to the reporter, and they say the whole thing looked about as American as it gets until the guy came out to touch up some of the paint. Wasn't used to the attention or something, I suppose, or he never planned on it, and people kept on wanting to talk to him, but all he did was put his head down or nod all shy, and he didn't say nothing amidst all kinds of shouting and a whole lot of why'd you do it, Fred, and now that I think of it, I can't even remember his name. But the reporter, she finally managed to get herself on inside to his kitchen table. The wife made tea. Scones, the reporter said. Raspberry, and not from no pack, either, and the guy must have been a little more at ease, or maybe it was the Jack & 7 he was working on, and she asked him what the plan was. As in, was he gonna build a little monument and charge to see it, and maybe it'd be five dollars for parking and three for souvenir photos, or maybe he could sell it to some art fair or museum, and, just look-ing at the rig and having some knowledge of aviation his-tory, she said they'd love it at Kitty Hawk, or that place up in Oshkosh, or even the Surf itself, and the guy kind of blinked and looked up at this water stain on the ceiling. Said he'd love to put an engine in it and finish that last February flight to Fargo, or just take the wings off and hitch the thing up to a trailer with a wide-load sticker and do the ol' 15 to 4 to 94 dance, but then some nights he thinks maybe that's wrong. Maybe what he oughta do is buy some of them laced-up fireworks or a whole lot of fertilizer from the Fleet Farm over in Mason City, and wouldn't that be poetic, and what he'd do then is just clear the premises and blow the whole thing to kingdom come. Leave the pieces scattered everywhere. Let all these tourists sort through the wreck, and I got half a mind to say that's probably the best way to end this story, isn't it? On account of it's as close as they'll ever get to the genuine article. It's their only chance to see the real, unadulterated thing.

Hook, Line, and Sinker

We're in the backyard looking for UFOs with these binoculars Uncle Bernie always said he took off some poor dead Charlie, but really, he probably got 'em on sale at the Surplus, and my brother tells me the other day he (meaning my brother, not Uncle Bernie) went fishing way out in Council Bluffs and caught a piranha. I ask him how big it was.

"Size of your head."

"Bet it nearly took your hand off," I say.

He spits on my shoe. Says he's never been more serious and shows me a photo. There *is* a fish in it. It's got teeth.

I never seen no piranha before, so how the fuck should I know, and so what I do is laugh and shake my head. "You got that from some pet store," I say, and you never told the truth in your whole goddamn life. Not about women and not about fish, and if you ain't gonna let me find these extraterrestrial assholes in peace and quiet, then it's about time you head on back inside.

He stares at me for a minute. Fists get balled. I'm bracing for impact, but all he does is slink away like some kind of beat-up dog, and he doesn't even slam the door. What he does is let it latch all quiet, and I sit there looking up at empty sky, and last week I head on up to see him, and we're both thinking about that time I can tell, but we don't say nothing. Just sit across the table shuffling cards, and you know he's gonna go to his grave thinking I'm worse than Judas when, really, none of it's anyone's fault but his own.

Winter Dance Land

The official name is the Winter Dance Land Resort & Convention Center, but most folks just call it the Buddy Hollywood, and they hold golf tournaments there. Seed conferences. Ag expos and sometimes these big outdoor rock concerts, and of course there's the boatload of special events. Weddings and the like. Family reunions. The parking lot fills with all kinds of license plates, and they say there's no place on earth you'd rather play road-trip bingo, and groups go wandering around in different-color T-shirts, and parents sit by the pool sipping drinks. Kids fly down waterslides. Sometimes, the older ones, they sort of weave their way off for some independent exploration, and there's one room on the property that's a little bit cordoned off and papered over with quarantine stickers, and the kids, they like to tell stories about it. They say Buddy Holly's corpse is in there. Or his ghost. There are dancing skeletons or music from nowhere, and the last kid to duck under them ropes never came back. Parents never saw him again, though sometimes, if you listen close, especially over by that ice machine right there, you can still hear him screaming. It might even sound like he's happy. Like he's doing some sort of shimmy or shuffle, and I dare you to go on inside. No, you asshole, I dare you, and the parents don't much worry about any of this because it's really their time, isn't it, and children have to learn to live on their own, and the children'll come back here with their kids one day, won't they. Years later. Decades, hopefully, and the smell of chlorine will take them right back, and it might as well be a goddamn bouquet of nostalgia, except that then they'll get the bill. The prices will have tripled. There'll be crowds. The front desk won't even give out free toothbrushes anymore, and the complimentary breakfast will now be a 15.99 buffet (but don't worry, kids under two eat for free!), and they'll wonder what the hell they ever saw in this place, this empty-prairie tourist trap, and what's with this whole fetishization of death and tragedy and plane crashes, especially, but then it'll be check-out time. Hugs in the lobby. The kids will get in the back seat crying and ask why they have to leave, and can we do this again next year, and those parents, those once-kids-themselves, they'll look in their rearviews and offer a kind of sigh. A sad little smile. They'll say, well, your mother, your father and I will have to talk it over, but right now we're thinking why wait a year, and maybe we'll get back even sooner, and it's really a shame we don't see your cousins more often, and what better place to celebrate. What better place for a party, even if it does cost an arm and a leg, and they'll never say so out loud, but the truth is they'll know it's not going to happen, and then, as they hit the highways and head back to Minneapolis or Chicago or Kansas City or Lubbock, the kids will fall asleep, and the folks'll hypnotize themselves with reflective paint and cornfields, and somewhere maybe around Albert Lea, they'll catch sight of the kids snoring away back there, or else just staring at screens, and a thought will occur. It will be about sinking, crashing, fields of debris. What it'll be is, is any of this something that can be avoided, and they'll probably think real hard for about a minute, while the radio is mostly static. A country song. Maybe one of those old-fashioned gospel preachers, and then their answer will be, well, no, probably not. And I bet we're all just falling from the sky, regardless. Arms flailing nearly wings. All the time and every day.

About the Author

BRETT BIEBEL is the author of *48 Blitz* and *Winter Dance Party*. His short fiction has been included in dozens of literary journals and anthologized by *Best Small Fictions* and *Best Microfiction*. It's also been listed as part of *Wigleaf*'s annual Top 50 Very Short Stories (2021). He writes and teaches in Illinois.

Acknowledgments

I am grateful to everyone who has previously published work from this collection. Thanks to:

After Happy Hour Review ("Eppley Airfield Honeymoon"), *Alien Magazine* ("Pilgrimage"), *Bending Genres* ("Beechcraft Bonanza"), *Bull* ("Five-Cent Redemption," "Summer Dance Party," and "Do No Harm"), *Cheat River Review* ("The Bloody Holly Story"), *Coastal Shelf* ("Food Court"), *Door Is a Jar* ("The Searchers"), *Emrys Journal* ("Races Run"), *Faultline Journal of Arts and Letters* ("Dead Letters"), *Flash Frog* ("Good Wood"), *Great Lakes Review* ("Narratology"), *Had* ("Lighthouse Inn #4"), *Hash Journal* ("Real American Prophets"), *Hobart* ("Winter Dance Party"), *Lily Poetry Review* ("Three Frog Night"), *Lost Balloon* ("The House on Highway 18, Probably October 1999"), *The McNeese Review* ("Revelation" and "The General Lee"), *MoonPark Review* ("Hang 'Em in the Sky"), *New World Writing Quarterly* ("Lighthouse Inn #6"), *OxMag* ("Great American Vacation"), *Stymie* ("Exposure Therapy"), *Third Point Press* ("Kayfabe"), *SmokeLong Quarterly* ("Midnight Shift"), *Split Rock Review* ("Heavy Water Brewing Company"), *Vestal Review* ("Not Fade Away"), *The Waking: Ruminate Online* ("Sanctuary City"), *Witness* ("Spin It Straight, Spin It True").

Alternating Current Press has been incredible to work with, and I'm so grateful to Leah Angstman for championing this collection. At every stage of the process, her work has made this book better. I am in awe of the work indie publishers do to support the literary arts and of you, dear reader, for keeping written narratives alive.

Augustana College provided funding that helped make this book possible. Thank you to them.

Mom and Dad, your humor and support keep me going. Thank you for the unending supply of both.

This book wouldn't be possible without that long weekend in Clear Lake, so a big thanks to Jen, Matt, Russ, and Mary for making that happen.

Meg, I owe you a thank you for all the things you bring to my life on a daily basis. I'm so glad to call you my wife and partner. I love you.

Eliza, I love your curiosity. Please keep asking questions, and please keep asking for stories. I'll tell them as long as I'm able. I'm grateful to be your dad.

Finally, so many of my teachers have inspired me to write. To Geoff and Scott and Cindy and Ken, to Aric and Mike and Matt and Janelle, to Nancy and Don, the world's better for all your lectures and lessons.

Colophon

The edition you are holding is the First Edition of this publication.

The cursive title is set in Abrupt, created by Akifatype. The secondary title font and all interior titles are set in Adibafih, created by StringLabs Creative Studio. The Alternating Current Press logo is set in Portmanteau, created by JLH Fonts. The page numbers are set in Avenir Book, created by Adrian Frutiger. All other text is set in Iowan Old Style, created by John Downer. All fonts used with permission and full commercial license; all rights reserved.

Cover jacket designed by Leah Angstman, with some elements by Supichaya Sookprasert of Neang Art, Krista Monique, Matthew Priest, and Mohamed Hassan. The plane crash image is public domain, courtesy the Civil Aeronautics Board. The Alternating Current lightbulb logo created by Leah Angstman, ©2013, 2023 Alternating Current.

Interior Buddy Holly ink-wash illustration by Leah Angstman, based on original c. 1957 public domain publicity photo for Brunswick Records. Ritchie Valens ink-wash illustration by Leah Angstman, based on the public domain 2015 gravesite image by Arthur Dark, extracted in detail for the public domain by Taph Madison, originally from the collection of the Michael Ochs Archive, purchased with full commercial license from Getty Images. The Big Bopper ink-wash illustration by Leah Angstman, based on the c. 1958 public domain publicity photo by Van Dyck issued by the General Artists Corporation. Interior black glasses illustration by Mohamed Hassan. All images used with permission; all rights reserved.

altcurrentpress.com